D1592713

# SUSIE

*Also by Marion Chesney*
*in Large Print:*

The Dreadful Debutante
The Glitter and the Gold
A Governess of Distinction
The Highland Countess
The Homecoming
The Marquis Takes a Bride
My Dear Duchess
The Savage Marquess

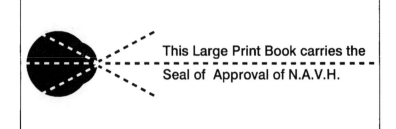

This Large Print Book carries the
Seal of Approval of N.A.V.H.

# SUSIE

# Marion Chesney

Thorndike Press • Waterville, Maine

Copyright © 1981 by Marion Chesney

All rights reserved.

Published in 2001 by arrangement with
Lowenstein Associates, Inc.

Thorndike Press Large Print Candlelight Series.

The tree indicium is a trademark of Thorndike Press.

The text of this Large Print edition is unabridged.
Other aspects of the book may vary from the original edition.

Set in 16 pt. Plantin by Minnie B. Raven.

Printed in the United States on permanent paper.

**Library of Congress Cataloging-in-Publication Data**

Chesney, Marion.
    Susie / Marion Chesney.
       p.  cm.
    ISBN 0-7862-3619-1 (lg. print : hc : alk. paper)
    1. Large type books.  I. Title.
  PR6053.H4535 S87 2001
   823'.914—dc21              2001041552

NEWARK PUBLIC LIBRARY
NEWARK, OHIO 43055-5087

*To the ladies of*
*President Street, Brooklyn . . .*
*God bless 'em!*

*Rachel Fevola, Elizabeth Cassarino,*
*Paula Mazze, Mary Nocerino,*
*Frances Puglisi, Ann Marie Parascondola,*
*and Rosemarie Sellitto.*

Large Print Che
Chesney, Marion.
Susie

696 6551

# Chapter One

It was not that Susie Burke didn't have dreams of her own. She would have been a very unusual seventeen-year-old if she did not. But her dreams were very much of this world, of the comfortable, jolly young man she would marry, of the cottage they would live in, of the sundial in their pocket-size garden, of the birds building nests in the thatch above their heads.

But her mother's dreams of the after-world never failed to embarrass her, and Mrs. Christina Burke's dreams were always stronger after church service.

As soon as she had unpinned her velour hat and handed her otter-skin coat to the parlormaid, she was off among the angels. The vicar, Mr. Pontifax, had preached a sermon on the death of a Mrs. Amy Bennet, a local washerwoman, famed for regular church attendance. Mrs. Bennet, the vicar had said, would surely now be in her well-earned place at the right hand of God, and this had troubled Mrs. Burke sorely, since she felt obscurely that that hallowed place was reserved for herself.

"I ask you, Susie," she began as she straightened her fringe of false curls, "do you really think one has to mix socially with one's inferiors in Heaven?" She rushed on before Susie could reply. "After all, the good Lord put us on this earth in our appointed stations, so why should He not do the same in His world? I would not know what to say to a woman like Amy Bennet.

"After all, good soul though she was, she was undoubtedly *common*. Christ says that His Father has 'many mansions.' Perhaps that means that the lower orders will be in one place and us in another. But then that does not seem very fair either, for surely well-bred people like ourselves, although middle-class in this world, have a right to mingle with the aristocracy in the next. I would so like to meet the Duke of Wellington and ask him whether he ever actually had an affair with Lady Shelley. I am sure he did not, of course, so the question would not be sinful. Nonetheless I cannot help feeling that Mr. Pontifax has become uncommonly Low.

"I had such a splendid wedding planned for you, Susie. I thought we might perhaps invite the Bellings to attend, for although

Mr. Belling is in tea, it is said he is a second cousin to the Marquess of Warminster, several times removed."

"I don't know how you can plan my wedding, Mama," Susie pointed out reasonably. "Not only am I not engaged to be married, but I am not even walking out with anyone."

Her mother swung around. "And neither you will, Susie Burke, if you do not make *some* push. Now, young Basil Bryant is calling this evening to speak to your papa. He is reading for the bar and may even be a judge. In fact, I am sure he *will* be a judge. I can see him sitting in the Old Bailey, solemnly putting the black cap on his head and sending some dreadful murderer to the gallows."

"As a matter of fact, so can I," said Susie dryly. She still remembered Basil as a spotty schoolboy who tormented little girls and cats.

"Well, then," said Mrs. Burke, brightening, "go and put on your blue silk and brush your hair well before he comes. You are so pretty, Susie — quite like myself as a girl — but so quiet and shy that nobody notices you. You may borrow my rouge, as your face is a little pale, but do not tell Papa. It is not necessary to bother him with these little sophistries.

"Dear me. Amy Bennet at the right hand of God. It doesn't bear thinking of!"

Susie escaped to the privacy of her room, and Mrs. Burke, finding that Susie had gone, wrenched her mind back to the everyday world and went in search of her husband.

Dr. Joseph Burke was sitting in his study, drinking a large glass of Wincarnis tonic wine and studying a sheaf of patients' bills. He was a thickset man with grizzled hair and a majestic sable beard of which he was inordinately proud. He had the reputation among his patients of being a very wise man, since he hardly ever said anything original, confining his remarks to clichés and platitudes. His patients, in the main, came from the overworked and underpaid classes and therefore were never in any mental condition to appreciate a witty doctor.

He was a good man in his way, and although snobbery was his ruling passion, he successfully managed to keep it to himself most of the time.

He and his wife were tolerably comfortable together. They had never been in love with each other, or anyone else for that matter, and therefore had nothing to be disappointed about.

He looked amiably enough at his wife, as he would have looked at a favorite piece of furniture — comfortably familiar, slightly worn, yet promising a good few years more service.

"I'm worried about Susie," said Mrs. Burke, pacing up and down the room so that her husband might admire her still-slim figure. At each turn she kicked out her taffeta skirts, which were edged with a deep border of fox fur. "She is still a child, admittedly, but she should already be thinking along the lines of an advantageous marriage."

"Quite so, Mrs. Burke," agreed her husband. "Marriages are not made in Heaven."

"Just as well," commented his wife irreverently. "I cannot help but feel that the Son of God was a teensy bit radical."

"Take not the name of the Lord thy God in vain," said Dr. Burke, taking another swig at his Wincarnis. Mrs. Burke gave him a mutinous look. She had long imagined her own entry into Heaven as a sort of presentation at court, and that wretched Mr. Pontifax had gone and spoiled it all.

"I shall sound out young Bryant this evening," said Dr. Burke ponderously. "I feel he is not indifferent to our Susie. Perhaps she would fare better if we arranged a marriage for her. She has no mind of her own. She is" — here he made a tremendous mental effort — "lying *fallow,* so to speak, and it is up to us to plant a seed therein."

"Exactly," agreed Mrs. Burke, struck anew by her husband's wisdom.

Upstairs, the subject of their discussion sat at her dressing table with her elbows propped on the glass top and stared at herself dreamily in the looking glass.

"Oh, you shouldn't say such things, Mr. Bryant," said Susie coyly, flirting with her reflection. Then she heaved a sigh. *It's no good,* she thought. *He'll always be horrible little Basil to me.*

Her reflection stared back at her in sad agreement, a serious girl with long nutmeg-brown hair and enormous golden-brown eyes in a heart-shaped face. Her dress was of a pretty and becoming shade of pink, but it was rather short, reaching only to her ankles, and had no waistline but a high yoke embellished with babyish frills. It was a suitable dress for a twelve-year-old girl going to a party, but for a seventeen-year-old miss it was decidedly unfortunate. Her hair was confined in two bunches tied with pink ribbons. The blue silk she was to wear that evening in honor of Basil was designed on similar lines.

12

The man she *really* would like to marry, thought Susie dreamily, would be very kind to animals. He would have a square, honest, homely face, and he would smoke a pipe under the old elm in the cottage garden in the evening while she leaned on the back of his chair. They would have a dog and two cats and perhaps some chickens. They would have a cow called Bluebell, who would wear a straw hat covered with roses in the summer. She could never imagine there being any children in her dream world. Susie was still too much of a child herself.

She rose and walked to the window, lifting the lace curtain and looking out. The roofs of Camberwell glittered in the winter sun.

There was something about a sunny Sunday winter's day in Camberwell that was the essence of boredom. Firstly, it was nearly Christmas and had no right to be sunny. It should be snowing, great thick white flakes, blanketing the drab world of rows and rows of identical Victorian houses stretching across the south of London. Secondly, since it was sunny, it had no right to be so bitterly cold. One of the chalky teeth of the gas fire had broken, and it whined dismally behind her in the room.

Susie had been fairly popular at school, but her closest friends had all seemed to move away to either the country or other parts of London. Her parents had paraded all the suitable young men of the suburb through their front parlor in a bewildering succession, but to Susie they all seemed strange and frightening.

Down below in the garden a few sooty sparrows bounced across the dull green lawn, still white in the shade with the unmelted morning's frost. A few old cabbage stalks were all that ornamented the vegetable bed, and a sulky-looking stunted sycamore crouched against the garden wall as if refusing to come out and play.

As Susie dreamed by the window the sky slowly changed from blue to milky white, then light gray, then dark gray.

*It's going to snow,* thought Susie. *Oh, please let it snow.*

It would snow and snow and snow, she decided, great white drifts up to the tops of the houses. Basil Bryant would not be able to call. They would have to live on the stores they had in the house, just as if they were on a desert island.

It would only snow on this small section of Camberwell, of course, so that the whole world would hear about it and scan their newspapers for word of the survivors. A large Saint Bernard would be brought from Switzerland to find them.

The army would be called in to dig them out. They would dig a marvelous tunnel right up to the front door. It would swing open. A pleasant, homely young man smoking a pipe would stand there. He would say, "Miss Burke, I represent the *Daily Mail*, and I want your photograph for my newspaper. You are very beautiful." And he would come in, and they would talk, and there would be no one to chaperon them because Mama and Papa would be sick with the — well, with the somethingorother that wasn't too serious — and it would snow again, so that he couldn't leave and neither could the Saint Bernard, thought Susie wistfully, for she had often longed to have a dog as a pet. And then he would ask her to marry him and all at once the snow would melt and all the bells would ring. "Beautiful survivor of the blizzard . . ." the papers would say as she was married. And . . .

And the bell sounded for tea.

Susie fiercely hugged her dream to herself. If she nursed it carefully, she could go on with the next installment at bedtime. But she had just been married. Oh, dear, she would have to start the dream all over again.

She managed successfully enough until the arrival later that evening of Basil Bryant. It wouldn't snow, he was sure. He was almost sure the wind had changed to the south, and if anything it would rain. He had an irritating habit of stabbing his forefinger to emphasize each point. He had grown out of his spots and into a small toothbrush mustache. He had a very thin, very prominent nose and large liquid-brown eyes. A prominent Adam's apple bobbed up and down above his hard celluloid collar. He stood with his back to the fire and delivered his case against the arrival of snow, bringing forward *Old Moore's Almanack* and his mother's left hip bone — susceptible to weather change — as witnesses for the defense. He had put too much macassar oil on his hair, and it gleamed wetly in the gaslight.

He finished his summing up. The case rested. The jury in the form of Dr. and Mrs. Burke agreed with him heartily. Not guilty of snow.

Susie's dream world of reporter and snow drifts and a Saint Bernard and marriage and fame crumbled. She was back in the real world. She simply must find another dream before bedtime.

Mr. Bryant was addressing her. "I say, Miss Burke," he cried, while his long, bony forefinger with its bitten nail went stab-stab-stab, "you look prettier every day. Almost a young woman."

"Almost a young woman of a *marriageable* age," said Mrs. Burke archly. "Susie was very clever at school. We hope she will marry a clever man, someone like, say . . . a lawyer?"

Susie winced at her mother's pushing ways, but Mr. Bryant seemed to find nothing amiss. He was warmed by the fire and mellowed by Dr. Burke's old port. "Lawyers make the best husbands, Miss Burke," he said (stab-stab-stab). "And one young fellow, quite near to you at this moment, Miss Burke, has ambitions to rise in his profession."

"Ah, well," said Dr. Burke, smiling, "every cloud has a silver lining, and it's an ill wind that bloweth no man to good."

Susie stared at the window. Through a gap in the drawn curtains she could see the iron lamppost with its flaring gaslight. As she watched, one snowflake drifted slowly down, then another, and then another. While Mr. Bryant elaborated on his ambitions, she stared, mesmerized, at the little patch of light on the street outside. Faster the snowflakes fell and faster, until the gaslight was only a soft glow behind a curtain of white.

"It's snowing!" she cried, unaware that she had interrupted Mr. Bryant's progress to the top of the legal tree.

Mrs. Burke's eyes looked daggers at her daughter, but she forced a thin smile and said archly, "Quite a child, our little Susan. Why, I would not be at all surprised to find out she still believed in Father Christmas!"

"Everyone knows Father Christmas does not exist," said Dr. Burke ponderously and unnecessarily.

As if to contradict him, there was the sound of muffled hooves on the street outside and the jingle of a harness.

A carriage came to a stop in front of the house.

Then the doorbell clanged.

"You had better answer it, Dr. Burke," said his wife. "Probably one of your patients. It's Rosie's night off." Rosie was the parlormaid.

"How dare they!" grumbled the doctor. "Everyone knows I do not practice on the holy day."

"Even Christian principles?" asked Susie wickedly. "What about the Good Samaritan?"

"Watch your tongue, miss," said her father, too startled at his daughter's impertinence to be anything other than amazed. "Had it been a Sunday, then let me tell you, Susie, the Good Samaritan would have done nothing about it."

The bell clanged again.

Dr. Burke opened the door.

Two liveried servants stood on the already whitening step, supporting a heavy middle-aged man who appeared to be unconscious.

"Carriage overturned, Doctor," said one. "Think he's broke his leg."

"I cannot do anything about it on a Sunday," said Dr. Burke testily. "You have your carriage I see. You will just have to convey him to the nearest hospital."

"Come along, Charlie," groaned one of the servants. "Let's do as he says and get my lord back in the carriage."

The swirling snowflakes momentarily thinned, and in the light of the streetlamp Dr. Burke's widening eyes made out the gold of a crest on the side of the carriage.

"My lord?" he queried, suddenly flushed and excited. "My lord?"

"That's right, Doctor," said the servant called Charlie. "This here is the Earl of Blackhall. Carriage got rammed by a coal

19

cart and overturned."

Dr. Burke took a deep breath. "My dear," he called to his wife. "Prepare a bedchamber immediately. We have a patient.

"The Earl of Blackhall, my dear! The Earl of Blackhall!"

# Chapter Two

There was no homely, pleasant reporter marooned with Susie during the blizzard. Instead there was a middle-aged lecher by the name of Peter, Earl of Blackhall.

Lord Blackhall proved to be suffering from a sprained ankle rather than a broken leg. He passed his days between the best bedroom and the front parlor, running up an enormous wine merchant's bill, which Dr. and Mrs. Burke gladly paid. They would have served him with fricassee of larks' tongues had he asked.

The vicar, Mr. Pontifax, when he called, had taken an instant dislike to my lord. He was shocked at the way the Burkes waited on him hand and foot. But Mrs. Burke would not listen to the vicar. Mr. Pontifax, after all, could not be trusted. Had he not said only the other day that Amy Bennet would sit on the right hand of God?

She informed Mr. Pontifax stiffly that she at least knew the honor due to her betters. Mr. Pontifax countered by saying that one's betters need not necessarily be the members of the aristocracy, at which Mrs. Burke became somewhat hysterical and accused the vicar of being a Bolshevist.

The irksome Mr. Pontifax being thus routed, Mrs. Burke had the leisure to fawn on her noble guest and nurse her dreams. The earl was not exactly in the first bloom of youth. In fact, he was fifty-five and had seen three wives into their graves.

In her fantasies Mrs. Burke imagined the earl dying peacefully in the best bedroom. His soul would naturally receive a royal welcome at the pearly gates, and she could hear the earl telling St. Peter that he owed the comfort of his last moments to none other than Mrs. Christina Burke.

But on the third day of the earl's stay, Mrs. Burke's dreams took a more realistic direction. For there was no denying that his lordship had formed a *tendre* for Susie.

Now, had Lord Blackhall been a greengrocer, Mrs. Burke would have been the first to be shocked at the idea of fifty-five matched with sweet seventeen. But the more the bloated lord ogled her daughter, the more she thought him a remarkably young-looking man for his years.

At last she plucked up courage to confide her ambitions to her husband.

"Well, well," said Dr. Burke, taking off

his reading spectacles and polishing them carefully. "I cannot say I am surprised at your ambitions, Mrs. Burke. I cannot say I am surprised at all. My own thoughts have been running along those lines somewhat. 'It is better to be an old man's darling than a young man's warling,' as the Good Book says."

The Good Book had said nothing of the kind, but Dr. Burke assumed all quotations came from the Bible.

He suddenly frowned as he felt an uneasy feeling somewhere in the region of his waistcoat. Dr. Burke was actually suffering from a guilty conscience, but he put it down to a twinge of indigestion.

His wife saw the frown and hastened to put her point across.

"It is not as if Susie will ever make up her own mind. She is so very shy. She needs an older man to take care of her. Just think, Dr. Burke, our Susie a countess!"

The word "countess" banished the last of Dr. Burke's twinges. "I do not know how long Lord Blackhall is staying," he said. "But we will not say anything to Susie about this. We shall just throw them together a little bit more."

And so it was that when Susie entered

the front parlor for afternoon tea, she was to find the earl alone. She shrank back, but the earl had already seen her.

"Come forward, my pet," he said, leering awfully. "Nobody here but me."

Susie wanted more than anything to run away. His lordship was a thick, heavy, coarse man with a bulbous nose, a waxed mustache, and protruding, red-veined eyes. He was wearing a smoking jacket and clutching a fat cigar between his fingers. The backs of his red hands were covered with coarse black hair.

Susie sat down on the edge of a chair next to the tea table. The earl sprawled in an armchair opposite, with his sprained foot up on a small tapestry stool.

Susie was frightened of him. She was frightened because he belonged to that mysterious top class. She was frightened to offend him and watched her table manners carefully. She felt guilty because she longed for the day when he would drive off. She hated the way his eyes slid over her body but put it down to a peculiar mannerism of the aristocracy.

"The snow has stopped," observed the earl, fingering the waxed ends of his mustache.

"Indeed yes," said Susie, staring down at

the tea table while the earl admired the shadow of her long lashes on her cheeks.

"So," went on his lordship, accepting a cup of tea, "I feel I must be on my way, although I'll be sorry to leave. I didn't know people like you lived in such style."

"We don't normally," said Susie quietly. "My parents are very generous to their guests." She plucked up her courage. "When are you leaving, my lord?"

"Ah, can't bear to lose me, my pretty puss." He leaned forward and grasped her hand. Susie let her hand lie in his while her large eyes flew to left and right, looking for a means of escape, and a barely hidden look of repugnance crossed her face.

Lord Blackhall noticed the expression of distaste on her face and felt the way her hand trembled in his own. He felt an almost heady excitement. He liked them when they shrank before him. It added a certain piquancy to the conquest.

He squeezed her hand tightly. "I think I shall take you with me when I leave."

"I beg you, my lord," quavered Susie, tugging her hand away. Her eyes flew to the window. "Oh, goodness. There is Mr. Bryant."

Never had Susie been so grateful to see Basil Bryant. The parlormaid ushered him in. He presented Susie with a bunch of flowers and the earl with a bottle of vintage claret.

He blinked slightly at Susie's radiant smile and pulled a chair up to the table and sat down.

"Well, I suppose you'll soon be on your way, my lord," he said cheerfully (stab-stab-stab), "I have it on the best authority that the roads are clear. Your estate, I believe, lies on the Essex coast."

"Don't point. It's rude," said the earl, stubbing his cigar out on the cake plate and ravishing a meringue in the process. Basil blushed and hitched his thumbs in his waistcoat.

"I say, my lord," pursued Basil. "I saw a picture of Blackhall Castle. It looks very grand."

The earl to all intents and purposes fell deaf.

"Sun's beginning to shine, my lord," said Basil in a very loud voice. The earl suddenly hauled himself to his feet and, without another word, limped from the room.

"He's a rum sort of cove," commented Basil anxiously. "Did I say something to offend him?"

Susie shook her head. "He's not very

easy to get along with," she confided shyly.

Basil hitched his chair closer.

"I say, Miss Burke," he said, taking his thumbs from his waistcoat, and his finger, like a spring released, immediately began its stabbing motions in the air. "I think your noble guest is sweet on you."

"He's old enough to be my grandfather!" exclaimed Susie.

"Quite," agreed Basil. "But it's brought you to my notice, Miss Burke. You're very pretty." And for the second time that day, Susie found her hand being held.

*"Mr. Bryant!"*

Mrs. Burke stood at the double doors that separated the back parlor from the front, holding on to the red plush portiere with one thin, trembling hand. "How *dare* you make overtures to my daughter! And unchaperoned, too."

Basil leapt to his feet and immediately began to state his case for the defense. "When I entered this room, Mrs. Burke," he exclaimed hotly, "Lord Blackhall was already here with Miss Burke, *unchaperoned.*"

"That is not the same. Lord Blackhall is a gentleman, a member of the aristocracy, and old enough to be Susie's grandfather!" retorted Mrs. Burke, and then bit her lip,

27

for that was not what she had intended to say at all. His lordship was closeted in the study with Dr. Burke, and already she saw her daughter as a countess.

"You led me to believe that any intentions of mine toward Miss Burke would be more than welcome," said Basil, beginning to pace up and down the room.

"Please stand still and listen to me, Mr. Bryant," said Mrs. Burke, trying to control her anger. "You have obviously misinterpreted my husband's kindness toward a young man. He has honored you with his hospitality, and that hospitality you have abused. You are a masher, sir!"

She tugged the bell impatiently.

Basil opened his mouth to reply but the fight had gone out of him. He began to feel that perhaps Mrs. Burke was right. Susie did not help a bit either, sitting quietly at the table with her head lowered.

After what seemed an age, Rosie, the parlormaid, eventually answered the summons, hobbling slowly into the room and complaining bitterly about her "haricot veins," which she said were bothering her something awful.

Basil tried to stumble out something in the way of an apology, but Mrs. Burke merely clutched the portiere with one hand

and pointed toward the door with the other in a gesture worthy of Sarah Bernhardt.

Basil made a last try. He turned and looked down at Susie. "I'm jolly sorry if I offended you, Miss Burke. After all —" He broke off in confusion, for Susie had raised her head and had stared straight at him with such a world of pain and bewilderment in her eyes that he recoiled before a depth of emotion utterly and completely alien to him.

There was a long silence in the room after he had left. "Mrs. Burke!" suddenly came the voice of her husband from the study. *"Mrs. Burke!"*

Mrs. Burke fled, and Susie sat by the table, very still. She had a feeling that something awful was about to happen, something so awful that her mind shrank from trying to sort out what it could be.

All too soon she was to know.

Rosie of the haricot veins appeared with the information that Miss Burke was wanted in the study immediately.

Now, the Burkes lived in quite a large villa built in the middle of the last century. It had enough room to comfortably house three Burkes and three servants and, in a pinch, three guests. But that day, Susie felt as if the ground floor stretched for acres and acres as she slowly made her way to the study.

Step by slow step she crossed the shadowy hall with its diamonded squares of colored light from the stained-glass door. Past the umbrella stand, where the silver knob of her father's cane shone dully in the gloom; past the large brass pot of ornamental grass; past the framed steel engravings and the colored prints of *The Laughing Cavalier*, *The Blue Boy*, and *The Boyhood of Raleigh*. She stood with her hand on the knob of the study door, looking back in her mind on her life of uneventful days and quiet nights, and knew somehow that the minute she crossed the threshold of the study, she would be leaving them all behind.

She opened the door and went in.

Her parents had been sitting on either side of the small coal fire and rose as Susie entered. Dr. Burke looked smug, and Mrs. Burke was trembling with excitement as she had been trembling with rage such a short time ago.

"Come here, my child," said Mrs. Burke. "You are the luckiest girl in England. Lord Blackhall has asked Papa's permission to pay his addresses to you."

"Addresses?" said Susie numbly.

"You are to be *married,* my dear!" cried Mrs. Burke. "Our little Susie is to be a countess. I am ready to faint with excitement. And my lord was so understanding. He wants to be married very soon and very quietly, for, although the age difference means nothing to him, as I am sure it means nothing to you, he is frightened one of those trashy scandal sheets of Northcliffe's might not see it in the same way. You shall not have a white wedding, Susie, but think! You will live in a great castle, and you will be very, very rich."

Susie burst into tears.

Both parents surveyed her with extreme irritation. After all, what they were doing was no worse than the behavior of many parents in this year of 1908. Did not the little sons of wealthy merchants sob their hearts out at prestigious schools so that Papa could brag in the countinghouse about "my boy at Eton" or "my boy at Harrow"? Were not young girls, daily sacrificed at the altar of St. George's, Hanover Square, forced by their ambitious parents into unwelcome marriages? Like most of their kind, Dr. and Mrs. Burke viewed Susie as a sort of extension of themselves, as yet unformed, to be guided by them.

They were dizzy at the thought of their daughter marrying a title. The minute the earl had asked for Susie's hand in marriage, even Dr. Burke's qualms of conscience had fled.

He had no son to provide for him in his old age, therefore it was up to his daughter to provide a wealthy son-in-law. Ambition made him cruel, although he was normally a kind, if silly, man.

"Leave her to me, Mrs. Burke," he said, jerking his head toward the door. "She must have her position made clear to her."

Mrs. Burke smiled mistily and left, wondering how soon she could decently put on her hat and coat and go and tell the neighbors.

And Dr. Burke proceeded to make the matter very plain to his weeping daughter. She had no alternative. There was no room in his household for an undutiful daughter. If she did not accept the earl, then she would be turned out into the streets without a penny. She would no longer be his daughter. The earl was a trifle old, that he was prepared to admit. But the advice and loving care of an older man was just the thing a silly goose like Susie needed. She need not trouble to give the earl her reply that day. She should sleep on it, and that would restore her to a more intelligent frame of mind.

Now, Dr. Burke would certainly not have turned his daughter out into the streets, but Susie did not know this. Nonetheless she tried to beg and plead. The earl frightened her, she said through sobs. But her father was adamant.

"I am shocked. Utterly and completely shocked at your attitude, Susie. Go to your room and do not show your face downstairs until you are in a more reasonable frame of mind."

Still weeping, Susie trailed miserably up to her room. The earl was waiting at the top of the stairs. She averted her head, but not before she had seen the cold malice in his eyes.

In her room, she flung herself on the bed and cried until she could cry no more. She would need to marry the earl. There was simply nothing else she could do. She was not trained to work, and her shy and delicate soul shrank from the thought of trying to find work in the cruel and unknown world outside. She was to be sacrificed at the altar as if Christianity had never existed and she were living in older, darker, more pagan times where they seemed to have endless nasty rituals thought out for virgins.

The earl smiled to himself as he heard the muffled sound of sobs echoing along the corridor. She'd soon get over her grief. Women were all the same. He was very happy with the day's work. He was suffering from venereal disease, and all the chaps at the club, including himself, knew the one way to get rid of it was by sleeping with a virgin. Of course, he could have bought a virgin. But when he had seen Susie, he had known that no other girl would do. It would have to be marriage, so marriage it would be. Her childish features, combined with the unconsciously sensual movements of her immature body, excited him as he felt he had never been excited before. The fact that she would probably scream the place down on her wedding night and would not enjoy the experience one bit added spice to the situation. For the noble earl came from a long and ancient line of rapists, and the Blackhall features were to be seen spread over most of the countryside around his castle.

He did not plan to invite any of his relatives to the wedding. One of the chaps from the club could stand in as best man. The girl must not wear white. It would make him look too old. That mother of hers knew what was what. He had to get her to kit the girl out in something that made her look older.

He then dwelt long and pleasurably on what he believed would be the utter consternation of his present heir, his nephew, the Honorable Giles Warden. He, the earl, would have that little filly in foal as soon as possible. Giles was, however, irritatingly rich, having made a fortune on the Stock Exchange out of practically nothing. But he would not inherit the title, and it would be rich to see his damned arrogant face when he heard the news of the new Blackhall heir.

With the exception of Susie, the Burke household rejoiced that evening, and even the servants were allowed champagne.

# Chapter Three

Dr. Burke ran after the departing carriage and threw an old shoe. "Just for luck," he said, returning to his wife with a smile that did not meet his eyes. For Dr. and Mrs. Burke were a very worried couple. The marriage had not been what they had expected — not what they had expected at all.

In the first place, that irritating vicar, Mr. Pontifax, had refused to perform the ceremony. The earl had said blithely that he knew a chap who knew a chap who knew a priest in the City who would cheerfully do the business. Susie had meekly accepted his proposal in the presence of her parents. The earl had kissed her on the cheek and had then departed for his home in the country, informing the Burkes blithely that he would "see them on the day." Startled, Dr. Burke had asked what they were to do about the wedding rehearsal. No problem, the cheerful earl had said. He himself knew the ropes, having been at the altar three times before, but he would get the priest-chappie to pop down on the day before to tell Susie what she should do.

Snobbery and ambition, however, soon closed in to banish Dr. Burke and his wife's fears. Their neighbors were most terribly impressed, and that mattered more than the carping criticisms of Mr. Pontifax, who, after all, was the sort who believed that washerwomen had a right to the best seats in Heaven.

Although Harrods could have supplied a trousseau for just over seven pounds, Mrs. Burke insisted on ordering one from Debenhams for one hundred pounds. This included fifteen chemises, twelve camisoles, eight pairs of combinations, seventeen pairs of knickers, seventeen petticoats, a dozen nightdresses, two dressing gowns, dressing jackets and boudoir caps, two dozen handkerchiefs, a nightdress case, and three dozen of something referred to in a discreet whisper as "diaper towels."

Susie's wedding outfit was a green velvet suit, generously trimmed with fox fur and with an enormous fox fur hat and muff to match.

The "priest-chappie" duly appeared on the afternoon of the day before the wedding, exuding piety and a strong odor of gin. Susie carefully memorized her responses. She was thin and white-faced and living in a nightmare, but everyone put it down to premarital nerves with such force and vigor that Susie almost believed it herself.

The actual day of the wedding was the first time that Dr. and Mrs. Burke actually saw the church of St. Jude's. The day was steel-gray and blustery. The church crouched at the end of a small mean alley in one of the forgotten corners of the City of London. Inside, it smelled strongly of damp and disuse, old incense, paraffin, and gin.

There was no organist at the organ, no choir in the choir stalls, and no flowers on the altar. The priest-chappie seemed in perpetual danger of falling down, and he scrambled through the wedding ceremony at a bewildering rate. There were no guests apart from a loud and tipsy best man called Harry Spots, who actually refreshed himself from a small silver flask before Mrs. Burke's horrified eyes.

The happy couple had finally driven off in the earl's carriage, which was to take them to the station. Dr. and Mrs. Burke were left alone outside the church, unable to meet each other's eyes. Mrs. Burke still clutched a bag of rose petals in her hands, and as her fingers twisted nervously at the paper, the rose petals began to escape one by one, flying off down the street before the winter gale, twisting and turning and rising up above the mean houses as if searching desperately for summer.

"We have done our best for Susie," said Mrs. Burke firmly. "She ought to be very grateful to us." But her voice quavered and her eyes filled with tears. "I-I d-did think that Lord Blackhall would at least have allowed us t-to h-hold a w-wedding breakfast. Oh, dear, weddings always make me cry," she added defiantly.

Dr. Burke hailed a passing four-wheeler and held the door open for his wife. "Let's go home," he said heavily. "We shall feel much better when we're home."

A small urchin with a face of ageless evil barred his way. "I say, guv," said the boy. "Did yer see that old geezer what married that young bint? Cor! Some folk ud do anythink for money. That's what my dad allus says."

Dr. Burke cuffed the urchin over the ear and climbed in beside his wife, who had begun to cry in earnest. Mrs. Burke longed to return to the cozy envy of her neighbors so that she might feel all right within herself again.

★ ★ ★

Susie's husband had mercifully fallen asleep in the corner of a compartment in his private railway carriage. Susie turned her white face to the window, where the smoke from the engine of the train billowed out over the rows of houses. "Can't go back, *never* go back, can't go back, *never* go back," sang the wheels as they raced Susie out of London and across the winter countryside.

Fine snow began to blow across the long black lines of hedges and leafless trees. Susie remembered her dream of the homely but kind reporter and tried to conjure up another fantasy. But reality was too much present in the heavy snoring face of her husband opposite. She had had one, just one splendid dream as she had been borne inexorably toward the church. That some kind but homely young man would leap from the pews like young Lochinvar and would bear her off to that magic cottage where the sun always shone and the birds always sang.

But the priest had dribbled on with the service and only the wind sighing in the bells high above in the black steeple had rung out a faint, protesting peal.

*God does not exist,* thought Susie miserably. *I have done nothing, nothing in my life to deserve such a punishment as this.* Her husband let out a gurgling snore, and a faint line of saliva dripped from his mouth and shone like a snail's trail on his beefy chin.

Susie had no idea what the intimacies of the marriage bed entailed. Her mind could not even begin to think how babies were conceived. It was something to do with a man kissing you and that was all she knew.

Then as she stared at her husband an absolutely splendid and vivid fantasy began to take shape. He was very old, after all. He would slip in the snow as they left the train. He would fall under the train. She would cry out, of course, but no one would hear her. The wheels would slowly grind over his body, and she would scream and faint and be caught in the arms of the homely but kind young man who had happened to alight from the train at the same time. There would be shocked stories in the newspapers and pictures of her becomingly dressed in black. "Prostrate Widow . . ." She could see the headlines now.

The funeral service would be very imposing. Would they bury him at Westminster Abbey? Yes, decided Susie, they would. And . . . and . . . what is more,

41

King Edward would attend. He would press her hand and murmur that it was a tragedy that someone so beautiful should be widowed so young. She would be very rich and beautiful, and all the lords would be eager to marry her. But she would turn her back on them, for the homely young man was waiting at the cottage gate, a pipe clenched between his manly teeth and a dog called Rover gamboling at his heels. And . . .

"Nearly there," said the earl, rubbing the misted carriage window with his sleeve. "Won't be long."

Susie stared at him in a state of shock. She had, after all, just buried him.

"Can't go back, *never* go back, can't go back, *never* go back," sang the pitiless wheels.

The earl's brougham was drawn up on the station platform to await them. Susie blinked a little at the glory of the equipage and the splendid uniforms of the two footmen and stately coachman. The earl's town carriage had been downright shabby. Not only that, but the carriage he had promised to send to Camberwell to convey his bride and her parents to the church had never arrived and the anxious Burkes had had to hire a hansom.

Admittedly the earl stumbled on the platform, and Susie's heart leapt into her mouth, but he regained his balance and showed no signs of obliging her by toppling under the wheels of the train.

"There'll be a few of the family to meet you," said the earl, "but don't worry about 'em. They won't interfere with our fun and games." Although this last remark was accompanied by a leer, "fun and games" to Susie's innocent mind meant just that, and a little of her misery eased as she thought of possible charades and parlor games.

The snow had slackened off, although a few frosty flakes still drifted down from the lowering sky. The well-sprung carriage bowled smoothly along a metalled road. A harsh, moaning cry came from above, and Susie, craning her neck at the carriage window, saw three sea gulls wheeling against the winter sky.

"Are we near the sea?" she asked shyly.

"Right on the edge of it," said the earl.

"I've never seen the sea before."

"Well, you're going to see a lot of it now," barked her husband. "And a lot of me, heh, heh, heh."

Susie cowered slightly away from him, and his eyes gleamed.

"Here, give us a kiss," he said thickly.

43

Susie closed her eyes and submitted as his hot, wet mouth closed over her own. She felt she would suffocate; she felt she would be sick. At last he released her and looked at her with a grin. "You need a bit of warming up, my lass." He grinned. "But plenty of time for that when we get home."

*I think I might be able to put up with it,* thought Susie wildly, *if I just breathe through my nose and think of something else.*

The carriage rolled inexorably on through the snowy landscape.

Susie had remained in a fairly numbed state all through the days before the wedding. She was a dutiful girl, and she knew she must obey her parents. She had been told from the day of her birth that they knew what was best for her, and she had obeyed them without question. But she was emerging from her numbed state with all the resilience of youth and beginning to feel many twinges of uncertainty and panic.

She began to wonder whether her parents would actually have turned her out if she had rebelled against this marriage. She wondered uneasily whether she actually *liked* her parents, but this idea was so novel and so shocking that she quickly banished it.

The carriage came to a stop before a pair of high wrought-iron gates. The snow had begun to fall again in blinding sheets.

"Got here just in time," muttered the earl. "We'll soon be snowed in."

Susie could hardly see anything of her surroundings. They appeared to be making their way slowly up a long, narrow road that led through barren acres of grazing land.

After what seemed an age, her husband said, "There's Blackhall."

At that moment the snow thinned so that the castle seemed to leap out at them.

If Susie had been a debutante of the earl's class, she would certainly not have expected this grim medieval fortress with its high walls, drawbridge, and great rectangular keep of four stories, which seemed to stretch up to the very clouds. Very few of the aristocracy actually lived in castles these days, and if they did, they had certainly gone about modernizing them. To Susie, who only knew about castles from the illustrations in her school history books, it was more or less what she had expected, although when the great portcullis was lowered behind the carriage, she could not help wondering what kind of mentality it was that kept a medieval portcullis in working order.

There was a moat as well, still filled with water. They clattered past the square, somber gatehouse and the bailey and across another drawbridge — over a dry ditch this time — and through another courtyard, swinging around in front of the keep.

Susie felt she had left the modern world behind to enter an Old English world where the brutish face of her husband seemed entirely in place.

The earl stamped the snow from his boots and led the way into a great dark hall hung with ancient banners and tapestries. A great fire, big enough to roast an ox in, blazed and crackled in an enormous stone fireplace.

The servants were lined up in the hall to greet their new mistress. Susie kept her head down and murmured, "Pleased to meet you," in a timid whisper that earned her the contempt of the servants.

"That's enough of that," said the earl, pushing her away from the last servant. "Bring us something to drink. We'll have it in the rose chamber. Is my mother there?"

Susie felt a little breath of relief. His mother! She pictured a kindly white-haired lady who would look after her and perhaps talk gently to her in the evenings.

The rose chamber bore witness to the Blackhall's former allegiance to the Tudors, having faded red roses painted on its plastered walls. A stained-glass window set high up into the wall portrayed a particularly violent martyrdom in which a tanned saint in a bright blue robe was being burned to death at the stake amid a welter of crimson-red glass flames.

What furniture there was belonged to the red plush, overstuffed variety, rather like the furniture in Susie's home in Camberwell, and it looked very awkward in these austere surroundings, somewhat like a plump suburban family who had come on a sightseeing tour and had found themselves locked in for the night.

A tall, gaunt, leathery woman who seemed to have been made out of whipcord and leather got to her feet at their entrance, and Susie was pushed forward and introduced. A pair of cold gray eyes stared down at Susie. This, then, was the earl's mother, the Dowager Countess of Blackhall.

She was wearing a mannish riding dress with a white stock. Her gray hair was pulled severely back, and her thin lips opened to reveal surprisingly bad teeth.

"So you're Susie," said the senior Lady Blackhall.

Susie dropped a curtsy. "I'm ever so pleased to meet you," she whispered.

"What's this?" Her ladyship's voice was like a whiplash. "This girl is common, Peter. Common as dirt. At least the other ones were all of your own class." She waved her hand toward the wall behind her, and Susie found herself staring at the portraits of three young women.

"Are they all dead?" she asked, surprise and fright making her bold.

"Every single one of them," said her ladyship with a certain amount of satisfaction. "I told 'em I'd outlive them all, and I did. Well, I shall just have to make a silk purse out of a sow's ear, Susie. When you have settled in, I shall begin your training and turn you into a lady if it takes all night and all day."

"Hey, not all night," said the earl, leering.

His mother killed him with a glance. "I hope you made it clear to this girl's relatives, Peter, that she has got to have absolutely nothing to do with them from now on. Nip the suburban influence in the bud. You may call me Felicity, and I shall call you Susie, since I am as young in spirit as yourself. In fact, probably younger. Take off your wraps, girl, and warm yourself at the fire."

48

"Yes, Felicity," said Susie meekly. This was going to be worse than school! She felt tears welling up behind her eyes and fought to keep them back. "It's a very nice castle," she ventured. "I suppose you mean 'nice' in the common way," remarked Felicity. "Don't use it again unless you mean precise, punctilious, or scrupulous. But since I gather you are trying to say that the castle is agreeable and delightful, then I take leave to inform you that you are wrong. It is damp, cold, drafty, and damned inconvenient. It is cold in winter and cold in summer. Fortunately, I am in excellent health and able to cope with its rigors. Many are not, which is probably why Peter's last wives are now lying six feet under."

Susie fell silent. A burgeoning anger against the awful old autocrat was drying her tears.

A servant entered, carrying a tray laden with bottles and glasses. "I suppose you drink port," barked Felicity, motioning the servant to hand Susie a glass. Susie did not in fact drink anything stronger than lemonade but was frightened to say so.

Peter, Earl of Blackhall, and his mother fell to talking about people that Susie did not know, and she was left peacefully to sip her wine and study her three predecessors, who seemed to look down on her sadly from their heavy gilt frames.

Felicity finally turned her attention back to Susie. "You had better go to your rooms and change for dinner. The housekeeper will show you the way." She rang the bell, tugging at a frayed bell rope on the wall.

Susie followed the housekeeper up the long, winding stone stair and felt almost out of breath by the time they finally came to a halt. The bedrooms were obviously at the top of the keep.

The housekeeper, a plump, motherly snob called Mrs. Wight, pushed open a stout oak door. Susie was ushered in and then left to examine her new quarters. She was to learn that, apart from the hall, the rose chamber was about the biggest room in the castle. She found herself standing in a small, stuffy sitting room that led to a larger, freezing bedroom. In the bedroom a fairly big window had been let into the wall and was wide open, showing the snow drifting past outside. Susie crossed over and looked out, hoping for a glimpse of the sea, but found herself looking straight down into the bleak square of the inner courtyard. She shivered and tried to pull the window closed, but it would not budge.

*What on earth happens when the wind is on this side of the keep?* she wondered.

A door from the bedroom led to a small suite of rooms belonging to her husband. She retreated back to her sitting room, closing the door between it and the bedroom to shut off the blast of freezing air from the open window. She wanted to wash her face and hands, but the washstand and water cans were in the bedroom, and the water was probably frozen solid. Suddenly the fact that her husband had his own suite of rooms seemed to her infinitely heartening. Her parents shared a bed, that she knew. But now it seemed as if she would have her privacy. A cheerful coal fire crackled on the hearth, and a rose-shaded oil lamp gave the room an illusion of femininity and friendliness. There were old piles of romances on the shelves, unfinished embroidery in the workbox, and an old doll lying abandoned in the corner. Who had owned the doll? No child, surely. Perhaps one of the wives who had brought this comfort from her childhood days to this bleak castle.

Susie shivered and decided to change for dinner. Her clothes had already all been put away, no doubt by the efficient Mrs. Wight and her maids.

There was a scratching at the door, and a severe-looking, angular woman in a black silk dress entered. Susie arose and dropped her a curtsy, which brought a thin smile to this lady's lips.

"I am the Dowager Lady Blackhall's lady's maid, my lady," she said. "She has instructed me to aid you with your toilette. My name is Carter."

Susie summoned up her small stock of courage. The thought of having this disapproving woman brushing her hair and helping her into her clothes was too much to bear.

"I am quite used to looking after myself, Carter."

"I can see that," remarked Carter.

"Please leave," said Susie. Susie was so shocked by the maid's impertinence that it showed on her expressive face.

Carter retreated quickly after choking out a reluctant apology.

Susie gave a sigh of relief when the door closed behind Carter. Then she realized she did not know the time. The sky was now very dark outside. She supposed they would ring some bell or gong for dinner. But then how would she hear it up here at the top of the keep? She plucked up her courage and decided to change quickly and make her own way downstairs.

She chose a golden-brown velvet dinner gown trimmed with bands of sable. It was not fashionable for such a young girl, married or not, to wear fur, but Mrs. Burke had obeyed the earl's request and had tried to age her daughter.

The neckline was cut low over her bosom. She fastened a string of pearls around her neck and secured a few more pins in her hair, which was piled up on top of her head. Susie had been allowed to wear her hair up at last.

She opened the door to the passage and looked out. It was pitch-black. She walked back and opened the door of her bedroom, steeling herself against the icy blast from the open window, and picked up the candle from beside the bed. She lit it from the fire in her sitting room and, holding it high, ventured out into the stone passage again.

Susie could not remember from which direction she had come. She picked her way slowly along to the left and, after what seemed like ages, felt her way around a corner. A shaft of white moonlight cut across this new passage. She edged toward it.

An embrasure had been cut into the

great thickness of the castle wall, ending in a long, thin arrow slit that overlooked the raging, pounding, heaving, battling freedom of the sea.

The keep was perched on the top of a tall cliff. A small winter moon raced through the storm clouds over the glittering, turning water, and Susie stood fascinated, the flame of her candle flaring and streaming in the chill wind. She slowly put it down on a stone niche and moved closer to the arrow slit.

Susie had never seen the sea before, and this first glimpse took her breath away. It was exhilarating. She wanted to shout and sing and dance, but seventeen years of social restrictions would not let her.

She stood there for a very long time, staring at the tumbling water. Something seemed to loosen inside her, and she said aloud, "I *hate* him. I hate my husband, and I wish he were dead."

"Don't you want to be a countess?" asked a mocking voice behind her, and she swung around in fright with her hand to her mouth.

A young man stood looking at her in the moonlight. He was wearing evening dress, which hugged his slim, muscular figure. The moonlight washed the color from his eyes and face, but Susie noticed that his eyes were very long and slightly tilted and his hair was a close cap of tight silver curls. He had a firm but sensuous mouth, which at that moment was curved in a half smile. He looked like something out of Greek mythology, reflected Susie wildly. One of the beautiful, incalculable gods, forever mocking, forever cruel.

"You haven't answered my question," he said.

"I was quoting something," lied Susie. "A line from a school play, that is all."

"You would make a good actress," he said in a light, amused voice. "You put so much passion and fire into your lines, I really thought you meant them."

Susie picked up her candle. "You are blocking my way, sir. I am going downstairs to join my husband."

"You won't find him this way," he teased. "I had better escort you. Allow me to introduce myself. Giles Warden at your service, ma'am. And you, I gather, are Henry the Eighth's latest."

"Henry the . . ."

"My Uncle Peter. We call him Henry the Eighth, but don't worry, he doesn't behead his wives."

"I don't think this conversation is in very

good taste," remarked Susie, relieved to find they had reached the top of the stairs, where a lamp was burning on a small side table.

He took her candle from her and blew it out. "No, you are quite right," he said. "Very bad taste. But you see, you are so very young. I was impertinent. Forgive me?"

Susie looked up at him, seeing him properly for the first time in the lamplight. His hair was gold, not silver, and his eyes were a light blue. His heavy eyelids curved upward at the corners. He was extremely good-looking in a sensuous sort of Greek god way — that is if you like sensuous Greek gods, which Susie decided she most definitely did not. Witness what had happened to her breathing. It was quite ragged, and surely only people you didn't like had that sort of effect on your emotions.

"I forgive you," she said in a chilly little voice as she allowed him to lead her downstairs, wishing he would take his hand from under her arm, since it seemed to make it go numb and her knees go wobbly.

"Has Felicity been bullying you?" he asked pleasantly as they finally reached the hall.

Susie thought for a minute. Felicity had been unpleasant and patronizing, but in Susie's experience, so were most grown-up people. Susie did not yet feel grown-up herself and regarded everyone over twenty as being a potential parent. "No," she replied, stealing another look at her companion and trying to decide his age. Around thirty, she guessed, and sighed. That put him definitely in the parent class. He would no doubt start giving her orders along with the rest of them.

The earl was standing in front of the fireplace in the rose chamber. He had somehow managed to change into evening dress, probably when Susie had been standing watching the sea, for she certainly had not heard him moving about his rooms.

The earl glared at his nephew. "Trying to poach on my land already, what?"

"Wouldn't dream of it," drawled Giles, and Susie looked from one to the other, wondering what they were talking about.

Felicity was dressed from head to foot in black velvet ornamented with jet. Although she was a tall woman, the skirt of her dress trailed along the ground behind her, making her look like a singularly healthy ghoul. The reason for this was that Felicity never threw any of her clothes away, and the dress had been designed in her youth to cover a wide crinoline hoop. She had simply closeted the hoop and kept the dress.

"Why did you invite me here?" asked Giles as he accepted a glass of sherry from a footman.

"To put your stuck-up nose out of joint, that's why," said the earl, hitching up the tails of his evening coat. "Thought I was too old to marry, heh? Well, I ain't, and I ain't too old to father an heir either."

Giles swung around and studied Susie's face. Her eyes were wide and innocent. He felt a sudden qualm. *Why, I believe she still thinks that babies are found under gooseberry bushes,* he thought. *Well, she's in for a nasty awakening.*

"It doesn't matter to me who your heir is," he rejoined calmly. "I only wish I'd known that that was the so-called urgent reason for hailing me down to this drafty old dump. I'm not mad on titles, old boy, and I don't need your money, so why am I supposed to get upset?"

The earl stared at him in a temper, his red-veined eyes bulging out of his head.

"You damned sneering pup. I've always hated you and that dreary father of yours.

Him and his books and manuscripts. Never brought him any money, did it?"

"No," agreed Giles, "but then I have all the financial genius of the family. I'm really sickeningly rich, Uncle. Why, how funny and red your dear old face has gone, and I swear the wax is melting on your mustache."

"That's enough!" snapped Felicity. "I'll have my hands full enough with Susie without you two quarreling."

"What's Susie got to do with it?" asked Giles in surprise.

"She's got to be turned into a lady," said Felicity.

"Strange," murmured Giles, "she looks exactly like one to me."

Susie threw him a shy look of gratitude. Perhaps that perpetually mocking glint in Giles Warden's eyes was misleading. Perhaps he was kind.

She had expected the dining room to be a vast place with a mile-long table, but it was, in fact, rather small, almost as small as the dining room at Camberwell. It was one of the keep's prettier rooms, having a rose-patterned carpet to cover the stone floor and exquisite gold and green tapestries to cover the stone walls. Candles blazed everywhere, and the liveried footmen outnumbered the diners.

The food was reassuringly simple, the earl confining his gourmand taste to someone else's table. Susie was urged to drink up her wine by her husband but Felicity mercifully put a stop to that.

"What is the point in pouring good vintage wine down the throat of an untutored girl," she declared. "It's wasted on her."

It was to be one of Felicity's few maxims with which Susie found herself in total agreement. She thought the wine tasted like vinegar and had preferred the sweet taste of the port she had had earlier in the day.

Felicity turned her tormenting, restless attention to Giles. "And what about you?" she demanded. "When are you getting married again?"

Susie flinched. Married *again?* Were they all bluebeards?

"I'm not," said Giles calmly. "Once was enough."

"Did she die?" asked Susie sympathetically.

"No," said Giles. "She ran away to the South of France with an elderly colonel, who, I believe, beats her soundly every day."

"How horrible!"

"Not really," said Giles, looking amused. "I must have driven her mad. I treated her like spun glass and wrote poetry to her and brought her flowers and told her she was an angel from Heaven."

"But any woman would adore that," said Susie wonderingly.

"Not really," said Giles, helping himself to potatoes from a dish held by a footman. "She said I made her sick, so she rushed from my extreme to the colonel's extreme. She is happy in her way. Do not be sorry for her."

"I was feeling sorry for you," said Susie boldly.

He smiled into her eyes in a slow, caressing way. "There is no need, I assure you. It was a good lesson. I look at all women with the eyes of reality now. Even very pretty girls like yourself."

"You're all stupid," said Felicity. "A woman should be a companion to a man. Your father and I, Peter, used to hunt together and discuss the problems of the estate together. He had no secrets from me. We were pals."

"What about Flossie Hagger down in the village," said the earl cruelly. "You mean he didn't even keep *her* a secret?"

Felicity turned red. "I knew about that,

but it is a lady's first duty to turn a blind eye to her husband's peccadilloes."

"Hear that, Susie?" said her husband, laughing.

But Susie did not know what they were talking about.

At last it came time for the ladies to retire to the rose chamber and leave the gentlemen to their port.

There was a long silence after they had left. The earl toyed with his cigar cutter and thought of the pleasures of the night to come. There was nothing more exciting, he reflected, than making love to a girl in that bed beside the open window. It had been a long time, but he could almost experience the erotic thrill of the cold air on his naked back and the warm, struggling, and protesting girl underneath. Pleasure would surely be doubled this time, for he had bought a new interior spring mattress from Peel's in the Tottenham Court Road in honor of his wedding night.

Giles toyed with his glass and thought very uncomfortable thoughts. Never, he reflected, had he seen a girl so naive and so innocent. He wished his own rooms were on a different floor. He wished he could escape, but the servants had told him that the roads were blocked.

"Go easy with her, Uncle," he said at last. "She's so very young."

The earl looked at his nephew doubtfully. There had been a time when he, the earl, had almost had Farmer Bligh's youngest, but Giles had stepped in and threatened to horsewhip him if he so much as laid hands on the girl. The earl knew that Giles's slim figure was deceptive and that his beautifully tailored evening suit covered a formidable mass of muscle and sinew. What if he should interfere with tonight's pleasures?

Then Giles himself gave the earl an idea. "Where did you meet her?" Giles asked.

The earl had a brain wave. He tapped the side of his nose and grinned. "Stage door of The Follies," he said.

"What? Are you trying to tell me that that beautiful, innocent creature is a chorus girl?"

The earl nodded gleefully.

"Then why marry her?"

"Blackmail," said the earl. "I had her when she was a minor, see? I may not have been the only one, but her parents found out and made me sign a paper saying I would marry her when she came of age."

The earl lay back, watching with amusement the rare expression of shock on

Giles's face. Of course Giles would find out the whole thing was a tissue of lies, but by that time he should have had a few nights fun and that was all that mattered.

"She's a brilliant little actress," observed the earl eventually, breaking the silence. "More than me has fallen for that butter-wouldn't-melt-in-my-mouth act. Why, ask Chalmers! He would have married her himself if he could have."

"Chalmers is very wealthy. Why didn't she accept him and release you from your promise?"

"Chalmers ain't got a title," said the earl, "and my Susie had a mind to be a countess."

Now, Giles Warden had certainly known his uncle to lie. But he could not believe that his uncle would have the imagination to think up such a whopper as this. And Susie was not in the room. Seeing Susie through the distorting glass of the earl's imagination, Giles seemed to realize that all her innocent ways were the result of low cunning.

He felt depressed and sick.

"I shall not join you in the drawing room," he said wryly. "Have a good night."

"I shall, my boy," said the earl, grinning. "Oh, indeed I shall!"

★ ★ ★

A bare half hour later Susie crept shivering into bed. She had tried again to close the window without success and, although a fire was burning on the hearth, the room was unbearably cold, and the bed was pushed up against the window. As she huddled down under the blankets she realized the room was still lit by two bright oil lamps. She would need to crawl out and extinguish them.

She was just reaching to turn down the wick of the first lamp when the door from her husband's quarters opened and the earl bounded in.

He was stark naked.

Susie stared at him in terror. The only male nudity she had ever seen was a statue at the Royal Academy, and the muscular marble figure had worn only a fig leaf. But that handsome stone creature left her unprepared for the reality of a naked, hairy, middle-aged man with a peculiar appendage like a pump handle sticking out from his body.

"Come here!" said the earl thickly, stretching out his arms.

Susie shrank away from him, and then the pursuit began in earnest. She fled toward her sitting room, but the earl got there first and locked the bedroom door and threw the key out of the window.

Susie ran hither and thither about the room, pursued by her gleeful husband, who was uttering noises like battle cries.

He made a dive and nearly got her, and she jumped onto the bed and was bounced off again by the excellent spring of Mr. Peel's mattress and landed in a sobbing heap on the floor.

"Tally-ho!" yelled the earl, leaping high in the air and landing feetfirst on the bed with all his weight. His heavy bulk turned the bed into a veritable trampoline.

The steel springs uncoiled with a tremendous thrust and, before Susie's terrified eyes, the naked earl was catapulted straight out through the window.

"By Jove! . . ." were the last words he said.

In no time at all, there was a sickening *crrruuummp!* from the courtyard below.

Susie was a very wealthy widow.

# Chapter Four

The Earl of Blackhall was buried unwept, unhonored, and unsung, not in Westminster Abbey but in the family vault in the small churchyard in the village with the senior Lady Blackhall, Susie, and Giles the only relatives in attendance. The roads were too blocked with snow to allow any of the earl's other relatives to visit his graveside, even supposing they had wished to, for he had alienated the lot of them long ago.

The older servants, who might have mourned the passing of their lord, quickly dried their tears on learning that the earl had left all his vast fortune to his upstart wife, who was no better than she should be.

The servants who had been present when the earl had been telling Giles of Susie's disgraceful background had believed every word, and the grim murmur of "murder" could be heard whispering along the castle walls.

Giles was also troubled. He could not get the memory of Susie staring down at the sea and wishing her husband dead out of his mind.

He was almost relieved to return from the funeral and find the presence of a burly police inspector accompanied by the village constable waiting for him. Giles was now the Earl of Blackhall, and although he had not inherited the late peer's money, the castle and its grounds and land were now rightfully his.

The inspector introduced himself as a Mr. Disher. Giles led the policemen into a small library on the first floor of the keep and asked them their business.

Mr. Bertram Jones, the village constable, sat in a chair in the corner and took out a large pristine notebook and licked the stub of his pencil.

"Well, it's like this, my lord," said Inspector Disher awkwardly, removing his hard bowler and resting it on one plump knee. "We've been receiving anonymous letters about Lord Blackhall's death. Now, as you know, Dr. Edwards signed the death certificate and said it was an accident. But in view of these here letters . . ."

"This is distressing," said Giles. "I'll take you into my confidence, Inspector. My uncle married a very young girl and has left her his entire fortune. There were no bequests at all to the servants. He did not even leave his mother a penny. So my great-aunt and the servants feel his wife coerced him into making such a will, but I know my uncle was lazy and careless and would find it easier to leave the lot to one individual rather than splitting it. He was not the type of man to care what happened after his death. On the other hand, it would ease our minds if you went forward with your investigation. If Lady Blackhall is innocent, then she will be free from these hints and rumors." He did not say what might happen if she were proved guilty.

"I must insist," added Giles, "that no word of this gets into the newspapers. We have enough trouble without being besieged by reporters. We sent no announcement of my uncle's death to the press. The relatives were all informed by letter. Now, would you like to begin with me?"

"Very good, my lord," said Inspector Disher, stifling a little sigh of relief. This had been his first case in upper circles, so to speak, and he had been frightened of angry and irate aristocrats reporting him to the lord lieutenant of the county.

"At the time of the . . . er . . . accident, where were you, my lord?"

"I was in bed," said Giles slowly. "The castle walls are very thick, and I heard nothing until a maid knocked on my door and screamed that the mistress was crying and shouting and pounding on her bedroom door. I put on my dressing gown and found the door to my lady's bedroom locked. I entered her bedroom through a door leading from my uncle's suite of rooms. In her distress she must have forgotten that she could escape that way.

"She was crying and in a terrible state. She said my uncle had jumped on the bed, and the next thing she knew, he had vanished out of the window.

"My great-aunt, Felicity, then entered and said some unfortunate things, whereupon young Lady Blackhall was sick."

"Can you tell me what your aunt said?"

"I would rather not," replied Giles grimly. "Aunt Felicity prides herself on having nerves of steel and does not realize that in tragic circumstances she becomes as unhinged as the next woman."

"I shall ask her myself if you would prefer," said the inspector, and Giles nodded.

"Now, then, did the young bride say or do anything at all, my lord, that would lead you to suspect she had murder in mind?"

Giles vividly remembered the scene at the embrasure but found he could not bring himself to say anything.

But Inspector Disher noticed the slight hesitation and tucked it away in the back of his mind, which was already working furiously. Giles said, "No, nothing," and the inspector thought, *He's a handsome lad, this new lord, and the old one was a brute by all accounts. Maybe the bride and this lad put their heads together.*

Aloud, he said, "That will be all for the present, my lord. Before I see her ladyship I would like to question the butler. I will need to question the servants, you know."

"I'll send him to you," said Giles. "His name is Thomson."

After Giles had departed, Mr. Thomson made a slow and stately entrance. *If he weren't wearing butler's uniform,* thought the inspector, *I would take him for one of the lords.*

Mr. Thomson was a portly gentleman with a bland, superior face, silver hair, and a haughty manner.

His lordship's death was most unfortunate, he said, but he believed in getting to the bottom of things.

He had not been present immediately after the mur— er — accident. Two of his

71

footmen and a housemaid called Betsy had been immediately on the scene. He confirmed most of what Giles had said but managed to convey from his manner that he did not approve of her ladyship and suspected the worst.

Lady Felicity was next. Yes, she had said some harsh things to Susie, but the girl simply had to pull herself together. Girls of that class had such vulgar emotions.

"What class?" asked the inspector, wondering how he had the courage to ask this formidable lady one question.

Felicity always listened to servants' gossip, and so she related the tale of the blackmail and the stage door of The Follies.

With a sinking heart, Inspector Blackhall asked Felicity to send Lady Blackhall to him and, after the door had closed behind her, he turned to Mr. Jones, the village constable.

"Things are beginning to look black, Mr. Jones," he said gloomily, "I thought these letters would turn out to be just a lot of spite. But now all this about blackmail and forcing the earl to wed! I suppose this Lady Blackhall's one of them hard, painted floozies. You could tell from that butler that the servants don't think much of her."

"She sounds like a Scarlet Woman," said Mr. Jones with satisfaction. This was the most exciting moment of his life, and he was relishing it to the full. In his years as a village policeman he had hardly arrested anyone, except for an occasional tramp caught stealing or a drunk on Saturday night. He gazed around the library with great calflike eyes, storing up every detail to tell his wife.

There was a timid little knock on the door and Susie entered. Both men rose to their feet and stared at her in amazement. She had found a woman in the village to make her a black dress in time for the funeral. Its simple lines hugged her slight, immature figure. Her eyes were enormous in her white face, and her brown hair was pulled up into a demure little coronet on top of her head.

*She's a child!* thought the dazed inspector. *Only a child.*

"Sit down, my lady," he said, "and don't be afraid of me. No one suspects you of anything now. We simply want to get this matter straight. Now, first of all, give me your maiden name and the names of your mother and father."

"My name is Susie Burke," said Susie in an emotionless voice. "My parents are Dr. and Mrs. Burke of Ten Jubilee Crescent,

Camberwell, London. My father is a general practitioner."

The inspector blinked. "No connection with the stage, my lady?"

Susie looked at him in surprise, and then the faint ghost of a smile crossed her mouth. "Oh, no, Inspector. My parents do not approve of the theater."

"How did you meet your late husband?"

"He had an accident; his carriage overturned. His servants brought him to our house, and my mother and father looked after him. He only had a sprained ankle, but they were very impressed with his title." Again that faint smile.

"And he fell in love with you?"

"Yes, if that is love."

The inspector raised his bushy eyebrows. "You did wish to marry the earl?"

"Yes — that is, my parents told me I had to."

"I see. Now, my lady, perhaps you could take us to your room and show us exactly what happened. I am sorry to distress you, but I am afraid it is necessary."

"Very well," said Susie in a flat voice.

*She's a cool one*, thought Constable Jones.

*She's on the edge of a breakdown*, thought his inspector.

Susie led the way up the stone staircase,

which became narrower after the first landing, and they were walking in single file by the time they reached the top.

The inspector mopped his forehead. He had often wondered what it would be like to live in a castle, and now he thought he knew and, as he confided to his wife afterward, it "fair gave me the creeps."

The all-pervading chill of the old keep seemed to penetrate to his very marrow. Dimly he could hear the pounding of the sea on the cliffs, and the chill air blowing along the passage smelled of salt. A particularly nasty-looking ancestor glared at him with contempt from a painting hung on the wall at the top of the stairs.

"I haven't slept in this bedroom since my husband's accident," said Susie in that deadly flat voice. "I sleep in my husband's bedroom." She pushed open a low, heavy oak door and led them through a cheerful sitting room and then pushed open the door of her bedroom.

A frigid blast of air from the open window struck the party. "I tried to get the servants to close it," explained Susie, "but for some reason, they would not."

*Probably bloody-mindedness,* thought the inspector. He said, "Why was it you were locked in, my lady?"

Susie's pale face flushed. "Must I tell you?"

"Yes, my lady, everything is important."

Susie heaved a little sigh. "I was frightened, you see, and I was trying to get away from him, and he locked the bedroom door and threw the key out of the window. I forgot that I could have escaped through his rooms. I just ran round and round the bedroom, trying to escape."

"Why were you frightened of your husband?"

There was a long silence.

A sea gull screamed outside, raucous and mocking in the deadly stillness of the castle.

"He was naked," said Susie with the wild, timid look of a trapped animal.

"I quite understand, my lady," said the inspector gently, and indeed he felt he did. The late earl had not been a particularly lovely specimen, and this young girl struck him more and more as being painfully young and innocent. But that in itself might have unhinged her and driven her to murder.

"And then what happened?" he asked softly, motioning behind his back for Constable Jones to put away his notebook.

"Well, I jumped on the bed," said Susie,

"and fell off — here at the end, on the floor. My husband then jumped hard on the bed — it was a game to him, you see — and the next thing I knew, he had flown out of the window."

"Would you say he was about my build?"

Susie looked at the portly figure of the inspector and closed her eyes. She was trying not to imagine the inspector naked. "Yes," she said faintly.

"Very well, then, my lady. Now, if you will just lie down on the floor where you say you fell, and I will be the earl. Did he say anything?"

"He shouted, 'Tally-ho!' just before he jumped on the bed," said Susie.

The inspector fought down an insane desire to giggle.

"Please," begged Susie, "before we go on with this, please shut the window."

"Right you are, my lady," said the inspector cheerfully. He crawled across the bed, which was still up against the open window, and stretched up. It took all his strength, for the window had not been shut for some time, but at last the rotted sash cords gave way, and it came crashing down.

"Whew!" said Inspector Disher. "Afraid you'll need to get that repaired, my lady.

Now, just stay where you are. Where did your husband run from before he jumped on the bed?"

"Over there," said Susie, waving toward the far corner of the room.

"Right. With your permission, I'll just take off my jacket." The inspector suited the action to the word and revealed a dandyish side of his character in a pair of scarlet braces embroidered with Scottie dogs.

Susie closed her eyes.

"Here we go," said Inspector Disher. "Now, you watch closely, Mr. Jones. Tally-ho!"

He ran across the room and leaped full on the center of the bed, which dealt with him as it had dealt with the earl — but with one exception. He rebounded and crashed full into the closed window, which gave a protesting crack but otherwise held firm.

The inspector got down from the bed, feeling shaken, "It's a mercy you thought to ask me to close that window, my lady. This here bed's a death trap. What's the matter with good old-fashioned ticking? Well, Mr. Jones, that's that. An accidental death if ever there was one."

Bertram Jones closed his notebook and an almost sulky look crept over his moon-like face. He had had visions of standing in the dock at the Old Bailey, giving evidence in one of the most sensational murder trials of this century or the last.

Susie rose to her feet, looking white and ill. "You've had a rough time, my lady," said Inspector Disher sympathetically, middle-class speaking to middle-class. "Don't let these here servants push you around. It's a pity the roads are so bad. You need your ma and pa."

Susie suddenly thought of the safe girl-hood world of Camberwell and gulped.

"We'd best be going," the inspector went on. "I'll just have a word with his lordship, and then we'll be off."

The two policemen found Giles pacing the hall at the foot of the stairs. "Well?" he demanded.

"Innocent as a newborn babe," said the inspector. "And very much in need of a bit of loving kindness. I went through a recon-struction of the accident and, believe me, my lord, that's all it was — an accident."

"Thank you very much, Inspector," said Giles, noting, however, the gloomy look on the village constable's face. Had Susie's mock innocent appeal tricked the fatherly inspector?

Giles still believed Susie to be an ex-actress, and unfortunately the inspector said nothing to enlighten him.

And so it was when Giles entered the rose chamber a half an hour later and found Susie sitting meekly by the fire, he found himself becoming angry and suspicious.

Nonetheless he said politely, "It must be a great relief to you that the matter of my uncle's death has been cleared up."

"Indeed, yes," said Susie in a flat, dull voice, as if she did not care much one way or another. Enclosed by the heavy walls of the keep, she felt as if she were living in some medieval nightmare from which she would shortly wake to find herself safely back in her bed in Camberwell.

"And do you feel sorrow over your husband's death?" pursued Giles with an edge to his voice.

"Oh, y-yes," lied Susie, "I miss him very much," her voice sounding thin and false in her ears.

The nervous strain of the past few days mounted to breaking point in Giles's brain. Her false innocence combined with that immature sensuous body maddened him.

"If there's one thing I cannot bear, it's people who say one thing and think another. But with your training, you must be used to it."

"My training?" Susie looked at him all wide-eyed bewilderment.

He walked impatiently across the room to where she sat by the fire and looked down at her. "You may fool a lot of people, Lady Blackhall, but you do not fool me. I'm wise to you. So let us drop this farce."

Susie got to her feet. "I do not know what you are talking about, my lord," she said, still in that expressionless voice. "But I have stood enough this day. I am going to my room."

He caught hold of her arms in a painful grip, moved by some impulse he couldn't begin to fathom. She looked up at him with those enormous eyes, and her childish mouth trembled.

He pulled her close and bent his head, and his mouth closed savagely over hers. A wave of passion broke over the pair of them, and they kissed and kissed and kissed as if they could never stop, while the winter wind moaned around the old castle and the three wives of the late earl stared down with their painted eyes.

He suddenly shoved her roughly away from him.

"You tart!" he said, wiping his mouth with the back of his hand. "I must be mad!"

It was the final straw for poor Susie. She collapsed into the armchair by the fire and, covering her face with her hands, she wept bitterly for a youth and innocence that had seemed to have been snatched from her, from fear at the ever-encompassing walls of this gothic nightmare.

"Dr. and Mrs. Burke," announced Thomson, the butler, from the doorway.

Giles stared at the middle-aged couple, who stared back. They looked the epitome of suburban respectability. There was a long silence. A log crackled in the grate, and the tapestries moved gently on the walls, making the embroidered green and gold figures of the huntsmen seem to come to life.

Then Thomson gave a discreet cough. "My lady's parents, my lord."

Then the tableau sprang to life.

"Mama!" cried Susie pathetically, rushing into that lady's arms.

"My lord?" Dr. Burke strutted pompously forward. "This is a sad blow to our little girl. We were unable to get here sooner. The roads, you know."

In one blinding, awful moment Giles realized that all that his uncle had told him about Susie was a complete fabrication. The girl was as innocent as she looked.

He numbly rang for the housekeeper and told Mrs. Wight to prepare rooms for the unexpected guests. He watched the still weeping Susie being led off by her mother and turned his suddenly weary attention to Dr. Burke.

"Allow me to offer you a brandy, Doctor," he said. "You must be cold after your journey."

"Very kind of you, my lord," said Dr. Burke, beaming. "Very kind, my lord. Such thoughtfulness, my lord."

*Snob,* thought Giles, *but no blackmailer. Oh, dear!*

Upstairs, Mrs. Burke was in her element, sending servants flying hither and thither to fetch every comfort for her daughter, from stone hot water bottles to put at her feet to ice packs to put on her head.

The servants were inclined to be condescending, but got short shrift from Mrs. Burke. It was not for nothing that she had broken in several gauche parlormaids and a recalcitrant Camberwell cook-housekeeper. Bursting with energy despite her fatiguing journey, she lectured the sullen servants on the Christian duties of obedience and threatened them with the everlasting torments of hellfire should they disobey.

Felicity's acid lady's maid, who had nosed into Susie's bedroom out of curiosity, was roundly told to take her insolent face away and to take some powders for her liver, which was obviously disordered. Mrs. Burke was vulgar in the extreme, but she was magnificent, and Susie lay gratefully back against the cool, fresh linen of the pillows and let it all wash over her.

Eventually, after boring Giles with a long list of platitudes, Dr. Burke dropped in to say good night.

Downstairs, Giles paced nervously up and down with a replenished glass of brandy in his hand. Giles was no saint. He was a normal, healthy British aristocrat. Therefore he reacted normally to the discovery that he had behaved like a cad and that Susie's parents were respectable after all.

It was all the spineless girl's fault, he decided. Couldn't she have opened her silly mouth and *told* him something? How could she, mocked his conscience, when her mouth was so efficiently covered by your own?

"I am going abroad, that's what," said Giles, stamping on his conscience. "And I shall not return home until those middle-class morons have taken their leave. When

I return, I shall suggest that dear Susie should set up residence elsewhere, preferably as far away as possible, where she can sit out her widowhood and eventually marry some young fool who likes colorless little girls."

Then he wondered why he felt so depressed.

Upstairs, Susie pretended to fall asleep so that she could escape from the attentions of her parents. She was glad her mother was bullying the servants — both deserved the other. Over her seemingly sleeping body, the Burkes sat at either side of the bed and congratulated each other on how clever they had been. To hear them, one would think they had planned the earl's death and subsequent will.

"Our dear little girl — a widowed countess," sighed Mrs. Burke.

"Every cloud has a silver lining," agreed Dr. Burke. "You know, my dear, I feel it is our duty to stay with Susie as long as possible, until she gets over her shock."

"Oh, yes, indeed," said his wife complacently. "Just think! Susie is so rich. She will be able to travel, give balls and parties, be presented to His Majesty. Thus does God reward His followers."

*Rich?* thought Susie, turning this news

over in her brain. *Money!*

"We shall go *everywhere* with her, of course," said Dr. Burke. "After all, it's thanks to us that she has had this good fortune."

*Good fortune!* thought Susie dismally. *To have been frightened out of my wits. To have been sick with fear. To know that I cannot face society with such parents. Don't they* know *what these people are like? Giles, who kisses and mocks and torments and insults. Felicity, who bullies. I cannot trust my parents. If there is an ugly, senile, old lord somewhere, they will have me married as soon as ever I'm out of my widow's weeds.*

The ordeal she had just gone through might have given a more worldly girl brain fever. But to Susie's still-immature mind, they were all actors in some strange gothic play from which she might awake if she could escape them all. The tragedy of the earl's death and the subsequent investigation by the police had left her brain and feelings singularly untouched.

She was young and strong and healthy, and tomorrow was another day. She had forgotten her strange passion when Giles had kissed her. It had been wiped from her memory by his subsequent insult. She would be glad if she never saw him again.

"Tomorrow's another day," said Dr. Burke, rising to his feet and unconsciously echoing his daughter's thoughts. "Yes, I think we shall be at Blackhall Castle for quite a long time, my dear. Yes, yes, quite a *long* time."

But the doctor and his wife had reckoned without Felicity. She had arrived back late after visiting a neighbor who lived a mere thousand or so acres away. She was informed by Thomson of the arrival of Susie's parents, and learned that they were not low blackmailers but a respectable doctor and his overly religious wife.

She moved into battle first thing in the morning, and the poor Burkes fell before her first attack. For although Dr. and Mrs. Burke were snobs, Lady Felicity was an archsnob and had honed the art of snubbing and cutting in the best drawing rooms in London, where competition was fierce. After all, being at the top of the social tree does not stop one from being a frightful snob. There is, after all, no fun in being at the top if you cannot make sure that no one else gets there, especially a pushing couple of Camberwell suburbanites.

The Burkes pleaded that their daughter needed them. Lady Felicity pointed out that Susie's manners were deplorably common, and that it was for her own good that she be severed from her parents' low-class influence.

Mrs. Burke hinted at hellfire. Felicity retorted with a word that Mrs. Burke had up till then only seen written on walls and had often wondered about, but now she felt she knew what it meant.

Routed at last, chivied and hounded and humiliated, the Burkes were driven to the station after a mere three days visit.

Giles could have eased their humiliation, for he was not in the least afraid of Felicity and had always had a soft spot for the underdog. But Giles had left for France after persuading himself to take a well-earned holiday.

Had he stayed, Felicity and Susie would not have been left together, and the shocking tragedy would not have occurred.

But he was not clairvoyant. He was merely a handsome young man with a guilty conscience, who wanted to put as much mileage between himself and Susie as possible.

# Chapter Five

Winter held a firm grip on the south of England. A brief thaw in February had melted the snow. Then the wind had turned, hurling icy gales in from the sea; dry, frozen gales that whistled and sang through the hard, dry grass.

Like a sleeping princess, Susie remained immured in the strong walls of the keep, escaping occasionally from Felicity's harsh social training to lie on her bed and weave endless fantasies about that homely young man who would one day ride up to the castle walls to rescue her.

Dominated by Felicity's iron will, Susie never contemplated escaping by herself. Her late husband's man of business had paid her a visit and had taught her how to write checks for "pin money," and had advised her to charge everything else and have the bills sent to him.

Susie longed to buy some pretty dresses, but it was unthinkable that she should wear anything but black until at least a year of mourning had passed. She had been allowed to visit the local town of Barminster, draped in a heavy black crepe veil and accompanied by Felicity. She had been allowed to draw a small sum of money from the bank but had been unable to spend any of it, since Felicity found all her choices, such as a pretty fan or a smart black plush hat, "utterly common and frivolous."

*Everything seems to be damned as "utterly common,"* thought poor Susie. *Oh, that I had stayed in Camberwell and maybe had married someone comfortable like the grocer's boy.*

But she hadn't, and she had therefore gained Lady Felicity as a mother-in-law.

Little did Susie know that Felicity had reluctantly to admit that Susie was coming along very nicely indeed. She still said "theeter" instead of theater, "blouse" instead of bloose, and "chariot" instead of charrot. But she had stopped saying "ever so" and pronouncing really, "reelly." Obscurely alarmed that she might no longer have anything to bully Susie about, Felicity started on about the servants one cold, bleak day when both women were warming their feet at the fire in the rose chamber.

"I could *order* them to treat you with respect, of course," said Felicity grimly. "But respect from servants is something that must be earned."

"Perhaps," replied Susie hesitantly, "they feel they are following your example."

"What do you mean, girl?"

"I — I m-mean," stuttered Susie, "I know you have my best interests at heart, b-but the s-servants hear you ordering me about, and therefore — just perhaps, you know — that makes them think that I am not a person to be treated with respect."

"Balderdash!" said Lady Felicity vehemently, and then quickly changed the subject, for she privately felt that there might be some truth in what Susie had said. "We will continue your education in good vintages," said Felicity. "Go down to the cellar and bring back a bottle of *good* vintage claret."

"Very well," said Susie meekly, all the fight going out of her.

She left the room only to return some minutes later.

"The cellar door is locked," she said, "and I can't find the key anywhere. I can't find Thomson or any of the servants."

"Wait a minute," said Felicity, striding over to an old escritoire in the corner and jerking open the drawer. "I keep a few spare keys here. Ah, this is the one. Don't lose it."

Susie took the huge key, which weighed a ton, and wondered how anyone could be supposed to lose a monster like that.

She then went back through the hall and along a stone passage leading off the far corner until she came to the cellar door. It took all her strength to turn the huge key in the lock, but at last the door swung silently open on well-oiled hinges.

Susie went silently down the stairs and paused in amazement halfway down. The cellar was ablaze with candles burning in various empty bottles. On the far wall a wine rack had been pushed aside to reveal an open door with steps leading downward. The cellar was full of the thud and boom of the sea. It was also full of every servant of Blackhall Castle and five rough-looking seamen who were rolling barrels into the center of the floor while Thomson, the butler, ticked off various items in a notebook.

Now, to a more sophisticated young lady, Thomson would simply have been checking a consignment of brandy from the wine merchants, which was being delivered by a hitherto-unsuspected door.

But to Susie, who lived more between the pages of romances and in her own fantasies these days than she did in the real world, the explanation was simple.

"Smugglers!" she cried, clapping her hands in childish delight.

The servants stood frozen with shock. Thomson's face was ashen.

"I'm sorry to interrupt you, Thomson," said Susie, "but perhaps you could find me a good bottle of vintage claret. I'm supposed to pick it myself, but perhaps this once, you could do it for me and not tell Lady Felicity."

"No, indeed, my lady," said Thomson, galvanized into action. He seized a bottle of Chateau Lafite less tenderly than he should and presented it to Susie.

"My lady," he said desperately. "My lady, *please* . . . that is . . . I mean to say . . . we should be *most* grateful if you did not mention this to Lady Felicity."

"Oh, no," said Susie innocently. "Smuggling is so very secret, is it not? I shall say nothing to anyone."

She tripped lightly up the stairs, swinging the bottle by the neck as if it were lemon squash.

The servants and smugglers waited in silence until she had gone.

"Well, I never," said Mrs. Wight, the housekeeper, collapsing onto a barrel.

"That was a close one," said Thomson,

mopping his brow.

"Think she'll keep mum?" grated one of the smugglers.

"Yes, God bless 'er," said Thomson fervently. "She won't tell. She's no more than a babe who thinks we're playing games.

"We've been a bit rough on her," he added slowly. "Reckon as how us ought to be extra polite to her. For she's not always going to think smuggling's a game like Hunt the Slipper or Forfeits."

And so it was that a very gratified Susie and a much-surprised Lady Felicity noticed the servants' change of demeanor. Lady Felicity's grim lady's maid, Carter, knocked at Susie's door before dinner and begged most humbly to be allowed to arrange Susie's hair and help her with her dress. Susie duly presented herself in the dining room, looking as elegant as a fashion plate and as beautiful as a spring day. Lady Felicity felt quite ill just looking at her. But it was the behavior of the servants that really made Lady Felicity jealous — a jealousy that was indirectly to lead to her death.

The servants were simply fawning on Susie, she thought sourly, so Felicity tried to think of some new way to make Susie feel inferior.

At last she hit on it.

"Do you ride?" she asked casually.

"No, not really," said Susie.

"Every lady should learn to ride," said Felicity grimly. "I shall teach you myself. We will begin your lessons tomorrow. I shall personally choose a mount for you."

"Very good of you, I'm sure," said Susie meekly.

"Good God!" said Felicity waspishly. "Have I not yet cured you of speaking like a scullery maid? Don't say 'I'm sure' at the end of a sentence like that."

"Very well, Felicity."

"I don't know why you never seem to listen to me," Felicity went on. "That dreary, common little face and that voice of yours get on my nerves."

Felicity intercepted a sympathetic look that Thomson threw at Susie, and this championship from a most unexpected quarter drove her to further lengths of bitchiness.

"I suppose a silly goose like you thinks a lady can be made overnight. But she can't! In fact, anyone from your class can only hope for a veneer of refinement. Underneath, they'll always be the same. Common as dirt. Just like your parents."

Now, there is just so much that even a

girl like Susie can take.

She rose to her feet and threw her napkin down on the table.

"Oh, shut up!" she said distinctly.

Felicity rose to her feet in a rage. "How dare —"

"Yes, I dare," shouted Susie, feeling all the rage and satisfaction of the turning worm. "Furthermore, I'm tired of your lectures. I wish you were dead, do you hear? Dead! Dead! Dead!"

"Go to your room," said Felicity, suddenly as cold as she had been hot. "I shall expect your apology in the morning."

Susie's fit of rebellion fizzled and died. She felt small and insecure and thoroughly ashamed of herself.

She trailed miserably up to her room.

She knew she would apologize to Felicity in the morning. She had not the courage left to do anything else.

Two footmen and a housemaid kindly brought the rest of her dinner up to her small sitting room. They banked up the fire, laid out her slippers, brought her up piping-hot cans of washing water, and Susie gave them a grateful, timid smile, which, as the housemaid, Gladys, told the rest of the servants later, "went right to 'er heart."

*I can't go on like this,* thought Susie miserably, *I wish I were dead.*

Then as she thought about dying she began to weave a romantic funeral for herself while a small smile began to play about her mouth. The service would be held at the village church. All the servants would cry. Lady Felicity would tear her hair and beat her bosom with remorse. She would throw herself on Susie's coffin and cry with grief. The vicar who would perform the service would be a homely young man with an honest, tanned face and blue eyes. "Weep, oh unfortunate woman!" he would admonish Felicity as he removed the pipe from between his manly teeth. "You and you alone are responsible for driving this child into the decline from which she died." A ray of sun would strike her coffin, and the manly vicar would begin to cry as well. "So young and so beautiful," he would sob. "Had she not been so far above me in social station, why, I might have married her and helped her escape from her dreadful life."

Nursing her fantasy and taking it carefully to bed, as a child would a favorite teddy bear, Susie soon fell into a dreamless sleep. She never once thought about Giles, Lord Blackhall.

Why should she?

She had nearly forgotten that he existed.

Giles, Earl of Blackhall, had, on the, other hand, not forgotten Susie. He had stayed with friends in Paris for a month and then had slowly drifted southward toward the sunny Mediterranean shore. The farther away from Blackhall Castle he traveled, the more it seemed to pull him back. It was his now, and there was so much to be done, so much land that could be farmed and was, at present, lying fallow. The moat could be drained, the keep modernized, made warmer, more comfortable. It was something to still have a castle to live in these days.

But still he traveled aimlessly on until one night in the garden of a villa in Nice, he kissed a very beautiful, very sophisticated, very passionate, and very willing lady and was deeply surprised that he should be unable to conjure up any answering response. While he pressed his lips against the warm face beneath his own, he remembered vividly the passion one kiss from Susie had aroused in him. He wondered urgently how she was and if she had forgiven him, realizing thoroughly and for the first time that she did have something to forgive.

He led the lady in his arms to a convenient summer house and performed his part with athletic expertise, while all the time his thoughts roamed homeward to the bleak castle on top of the steep cliffs above the roaring sea.

"Use your whip, you ninny! Use your whip!" But Susie would not.

It was her fifth riding lesson, and she was so bruised and battered, she could hardly stay on the vicious mount that Lady Felicity had deliberately chosen for her. The horse was called Dobbin and was anything but the docile animal that its pedestrian name conjured up. He had a nasty temper and a rolling eye. He did not want Susie on his back; he did not want any human on his back, and only endured Susie for brief stretches at a time because she fed him sugar lumps and spoke to him in a soft, pleading voice that somewhere in the back of his bad-tempered brain he rather liked.

Lady Felicity was herself a hard-bitten horsewoman, and prided herself on the fact that there wasn't a horse alive she couldn't ride.

During this, the fifth lesson, she and Susie were riding toward the steep edge of a gravel pit. The sky still lowered above them, and a dry, cold wind whipped across the rockstrewn moor. Felicity had become bored with Susie's torture and turned her attention instead to Susie's horse.

Suddenly she reined in her own mount. "It's time I showed you and that animal of yours how a horse should be mastered," she said. "Dismount and take my horse, and I'll take yours."

Susie gladly complied, climbing awkwardly up onto the back of Lady Felicity's more docile horse.

Felicity leapt nimbly into the sidesaddle on Dobbin's back, wrenched his mouth, and then lashed the animal viciously across the rump with her whip so that a thin trickle of blood ran down his flanks.

She then dug a wicked-looking spur hard into his side. "Gee-up!" she said.

And Dobbin did.

Right to the edge of the gravel pit he flew like an arrow from a bow, and right at the edge he dug in all four hooves and stopped short.

Lady Felicity went sailing over his head. Her astonished voice sailed back in the wind as she seemed to hang suspended for a moment over the gravel pit.

"Deary me . . . !" cried Lady Felicity.

And then she crashed down and down

and down and died instantly as her neck snapped on a convenient rock.

There was a great silence. Then a sea gull screamed overhead, and Susie began to shiver uncontrollably, climbing down from her horse and falling onto the ground, because her trembling legs could not support her.

After a time she gritted her teeth and, rising, made her way slowly and painfully down the steep sides of the gravel pit, her long skirts bunched over her arm.

There was no doubt about it — Lady Felicity was very much dead.

Susie began to laugh hysterically. Then she burst into stormy tears while a startled rabbit fled in fear from this peculiar human.

Susie sat down beside the still body and cried and cried, wrapping her head in her arms and rocking to and fro. This un-English manifestation of shock, this lack of stiff upper lip, was what kept her from having a complete breakdown.

Finally, after a long time she made her way slowly back to the castle on foot while Dobbin, now lazy and placid, strolled after her, accompanied by the other horse.

# Chapter Six

A year had passed since the death of Lady Felicity. Susie had recovered a long time ago from her shock, but still remained much the same dreamy, immature girl as ever.

Giles had thrown himself into plans for modernizing the castle, and workmen seemed to be hammering upstairs and downstairs morning, noon, and night. He had not had the energy or the inclination to find a home for Susie and had, instead, invited an elderly aunt to stay as a kind of chaperon. His aunt, Lady Matilda Warden, was a fanatical knitter, tatter, and stitcher, and trailed cheerfully from room to room of the keep with long, different-colored threads and skeins of wool hanging from her workbasket. She was extremely kind to Susie; that is, when she happened to notice her, which was about once a month, and Susie, in return, was very fond of the old lady.

The servants now treated Susie with nervous respect. They had not forgotten that Lady Felicity had died mysteriously, just shortly after Lady Susie Blackhall had wished her dead. The servants had, of course, conveyed their suspicions to Giles's valet, who in turn had told his master. But Giles had shrugged it off as gossip. He was too busy with his plans for the castle, and he did not mind Susie in the least so long as she did not get in his way.

Sometimes, however, he could not help wondering what there had been about Susie that had so attracted him and so repelled him at the same time on the night he had kissed her. Now, to him, she seemed like an ordinary girl — a bit vague and dreamy — but inoffensive for all that.

He had not even noticed that Susie, for all her vagueness, had taken on much of the direction that had once belonged to Lady Felicity. Susie must have been one of the few ladies of England in charge of a large staff who was not cheated in any way by the servants. They were too frightened of her to fiddle the books, and furthermore, she continued to turn a blind eye to their smuggling activities, at which they made a comfortable profit, Thomson taking the largest share, the housekeeper the next, and so on down to the little knife-boy, who had his meager wage augmented by a weekly smuggling bonus of three shillings.

Giles did not know anything of this. After all, he never went down to the cellars, and if he sometimes marveled at the excellence of the castle's vintages and rare brandies, he gave full credit to Thomson for having secured an excellent wine merchant.

He only saw Susie infrequently and then usually at dinner. He was too absorbed in his plans and alterations to pay her much attention, and Susie was usually lost in one of her rambling dreams. Susie was, in fact, happier than she had ever been in her life. Her housekeeping duties kept her occupied, and there was no one to bully her or make her feel small, and no scheming parents around to try to marry her off.

Dr. and Mrs. Burke had made a few brief visits to the castle but had not stayed long. The servants had not forgiven Mrs. Burke for her first visit's bullying and made life as uncomfortable for the Camberwell couple as they possibly could. Giles was always anxious to be rid of them as soon as possible, which he did by redesigning their rooms almost as soon as they had arrived, and Mrs. Burke's sermons and Dr. Burke's jolly platitudes and proverbs withered and died under a rain of plaster dust and an overwhelming odor of new paint.

Things might have drifted comfortably on like this for quite a long time, but that year, an early spring came to the Essex countryside. The air was full of birdsong, and the rich green of the fields was starred with wild flowers. Clumps of primroses shone in the dark shade of the hedgerows, and white and pink and red flowers foamed across the prickly hawthorn trees. On the gentler cliff slopes about half a mile from the castle, the soft haze of bluebells glowed gently under the tangled trees and bushes that scrambled their way down the rough surface of the cliffs to the edge of the sea.

The sea!

Susie stood one perfect day at a window high in the keep and looked wonderingly out at the infinity of blue and sparkling water. It turned and foamed and sparkled at the foot of the cliffs, and she suddenly felt as restless as the water such a long way beneath.

She went to her room and changed into an old skirt and a blouse and a pair of serviceable boots. She brushed out her long brown hair and then looked at the silk pads and bone pins and all the other impedimenta that she should put on her head and, instead, tied her hair back with a cherry-colored ribbon.

Hatless and feeling strangely free, she walked out of the shadowy hall of the keep and into the blazing sunshine of the inner courtyard. Then she went over the drawbridge, through the first portcullis — now never used — through the second courtyard, past the bailey, past the gatehouse, over the second drawbridge, where gardeners were working in the now-drained moat, spreading grass seed, and out over the green, green fields, where sheep placidly cropped the new grass and young lambs tottered and frolicked on legs as unsteady and as immature as Susie's dreamy mind.

She walked and walked until she came to the dark, tangled bluebell wood, which sloped precipitously down to the foaming sea. Heedless of the thorns and briars tugging at her long skirts, she scrambled down until she was standing on a smooth boulder at the edge of the water.

Her feet were hot and sore in their heavy boots, and the cool water looked very inviting. Susie took a quick look around, but there was no one to be seen, and who else would want to come to this lonely spot? she thought.

She opened her reticule and, taking out a button hook, proceeded to unfasten her boots. She unclipped her stockings from their suspenders; then, pinning up her skirt and layers of petticoats above her ankles, she sat down on the rock and slowly let her naked feet slide into the cool water.

She sat there for a long time, the sun reddening her white face to an unfashionably healthy, rosy glow and placing gold highlights in the streaming masses of nut-brown hair, which blew and tugged at the confinement of the frivolous scarlet ribbon.

After awhile her feet began to feel cold, so she raised them out of the water and stuck them out in front of her to dry.

That is how Giles, reining in his horse at the top of the cliff and looking straight down a sort of gulley that formed a channel through the trees and undergrowth, became aware for the first time that Susie, Countess of Blackhall, was possessed of a very neat pair of ankles indeed.

Now, Giles had seen quite a number of naked women, but like most healthy young Englishmen, he had to admit to himself that there was nothing more seductive than the glimpse of a well-turned ankle. Susie raised her arms high above her head and stretched with a fluid, catlike motion.

He began to wonder what she thought about, whether she was happy, what she thought of *him*. He was not used to being completely ignored by women, particularly pretty young girls, and for the first time, he felt a certain twinge of pique at Susie's undoubted lack of interest in him.

He debated whether to dismount and climb down the bank to join her. But then she would surely be embarrassed at being found in such a state of undress. He rode thoughtfully back toward the stables, beginning to wonder also about that rumor of murder. It was ridiculous, of course. But then *two* fatal accidents! *It's just as well she doesn't covet the castle,* he thought grimly, *or I should begin to worry about my welfare.*

He rubbed down his horse and was about to leave the cool darkness of the stables when a whinny from one of the loose boxes made him turn around. A horse with a long and unlovely face and a wicked eye was staring straight at him out of the gloom at the far end of the stables.

He called to the head groom. "Clifton! I say, Clifton!"

The bandy-legged figure of the groom

came hurrying up. "What is that?" demanded Giles, pointing at the evil-looking horse.

The head groom shuffled his boots in the straw and then said reluctantly, "That be Dobbin, my lord."

"Dobbin! *Dobbin?* You mean the horse that threw Lady Felicity? I thought he would have been shot as a matter of course!"

"Well, my lord," said Clifton, "it be like this. Your lordship didn't come back until three days after the death, just in time for the funeral. We had already asked Lady Susie what was to be done about the horse. My lady says, she says, 'Don't touch that there horse, Clifton. It ain't his fault,' she says. My lady do ride the beast often as she can, and I'll say one thing for my lady, there ain't a man or boy hereabouts could sit on that beast's back. We was going to get rid of him long ago, but Lady Felicity says with that laugh of hers that Dobbin was perfect for Lady Susie."

Giles stood frowning. First he was shocked that Lady Felicity should have put an untrained girl up on the back of a notoriously wicked horse; secondly he was shocked that Susie should keep an animal that had been instrumental in the death of his great-aunt; and thirdly he experienced a reluctant feeling of admiration for Susie from Camberwell, who should have learned how to ride such a mount.

"Very well, Clifton," he said, giving the groom a curt nod.

As Giles strode from the stables he wondered more and more about Susie. Surely that dreamy innocence must be a facade. Only a very tough girl could master a horse like that. He did not know that Susie had tamed Dobbin by kindness alone. Carrots and lump sugar and soft words and a soft hand caressing his nose had done what the lash of the whip, the curb of the bit, and the dig of the spur could not. Dobbin had been broken in by sentimental, middle-class kindness. He was, after all, a very common horse.

*Thank goodness,* thought Giles again, *she does not covet the castle.*

"One day this will all be yours, my son," said Susie to the golden-haired dream child who was sitting beside her on the rock. She had given birth to the child five years ago, she decided, but her homely and manly young husband had not lived to see his child's first birthday. He had died of — here Susie wrinkled her brow — typhoid.

No, too humdrum. Blindness — "You are my eyes, Susie." No, one didn't *die* from blindness. Killed in action on the North-West Frontier! That was it! Yes, killed in action and awarded the Victoria Cross posthumously. TO HIS WEEPING WIDOW, said the dream headlines. Poor Harold — that was her late husband's name — poor Harold, lying in a foreign grave under harsh blue skies while the vultures wheeled above, and his brave sepoys — were they sepoys? Must check Rudyard Kipling again — mourned his death. Now she was alone in the world with this beautiful child, who was sole heir to Blackhall Castle. Susie's pretty brow wrinkled again, But Giles was the heir. And what if he should marry? "I shall just have to kill him off," she said to herself.

Then she noticed that the sun was sinking in the sky and unless she hurried, she would be late for dinner.

Putting on her stockings and boots, picking up her reticule, and carrying her splendid dream with her, she hurried back to the castle.

Giles looked curiously at Susie across the dinner table. She was eating her food in a silent, absorbed kind of way. Lady Matilda had finished her plateful very

quickly as usual and was engaged in knitting some peculiar lumpy wool garment in
violent magenta. The fresh air and sunshine had given Susie's face a healthy
glow. Her hair, thanks to Carter, was ex-
quisitely dressed, and she was wearing a
lavender gown of half-mourning, which
was cut low on the bosom.

*She has a pretty neck as well as a good pair
of ankles,* he noticed with some surprise. *In
fact, she's a deuced pretty girl all round.*

"You are looking very beautiful this evening, Lady Susie," he said in a light,
charming voice.

"Oh, what? Did you speak to me?" said
Susie, trying to focus on him and hold
onto her dream at the same time.

"I said that you were looking very beautiful," Giles repeated patiently.

"Thank you," said Susie with a marked
lack of interest.

"Do you like the improvements to the
castle?"

"I beg your pardon?"

"I said, DO YOU LIKE THE
IMPROVEMENTS TO THE CASTLE?"

Susie twisted in her chair, noticing as if
for the first time the pretty paper on the
walls, the charming framed landscapes, the
fresh curtains at the windows, and the new

glittering Waterford chandelier, the crystals of which were reflected in the mahogany table.

"Oh, yes," replied Susie, half in and half out of the dream. "I was thinking of turning my old rooms into a nursery."

Giles dropped his fork with a clatter. "You don't mean . . . I mean you aren't . . . you can't be . . . ?"

"I mean I shall no doubt marry again," said Susie dreamily, briefly resurrecting her husband from his Indian grave, burying him again, and accepting the Victoria Cross. "The heir to Blackhall Castle must have fitting accommodation."

"The heir — Have you gone mad?" said Giles wrathfully. "If there is to be an heir, then I shall produce it, not you."

"How can you?" asked Susie as Lady Matilda's needles click-click-clicked. "Only women can produce children, or so I believe."

"Exactly," said Giles grimly. "I hope my future wife will do the job for me."

"Oh!" said Susie, wrinkling her brow. "But what if you die?"

Behind her, two footmen collided, and Thomson nervously dropped a wineglass.

"And just what is supposed to happen to me?" asked Giles in silky tones.

"I don't know," said Susie placidly. "I haven't thought of anything yet."

"More wine, my lord?" said Thomson in a quavering voice.

"Please, I need it," said Giles, still staring at Susie.

"You sound as if you are planning my death," he remarked, raising his glass.

Susie jerked her whole mind into the real world. "It's just my silly dreaming," she explained. "Pay no attention to me."

But Giles felt that the future of his direct line had been threatened. If he did not marry, and Susie did, then it would indeed mean that her son would inherit. This Camberwell miss's child would inherit all this, the home of his ancestors, his own name. Had he slaved and worked for a full year in order to supply some middle-class brat with a stately home? He had never before contemplated marrying again. Now he began to think he should get started on the project as soon as possible.

"I am going to give a ball," he said abruptly.

"Aren't all the rooms too small?" asked Susie.

"Yes, but I shall have marquees erected on the grounds."

"It will be an awful lot of work," said

Susie doubtfully. "I suppose I had better hire extra servants."

"What has it got to do with you?" asked Giles rudely. "This castle runs itself."

"Oh, no it doesn't," said Lady Matilda, emerging from her knitting and surprising them both by springing to Susie's defense.

"There's no one to beat Susie at housekeeping, except perhaps the late Duchess of Strawn," said Lady Matilda. "Place runs like clockwork; happy servants, good meals. Hadn't you noticed, you silly boy?"

"I am sorry. I was not aware you had done so much," said Giles stiffly. "But employ extra servants if you wish."

Susie looked at him shyly. "Will I be allowed to dance? I mean, am I out of mourning?"

"Yes," said Giles coldly. "That is, if you were ever in it."

Susie gave him a hurt look. Was another bully about to rear its ugly head? All of a sudden she remembered how he had kissed her, and looked down at the table. She had not looked at him fully since that night, and she had forgotten how very handsome he was. She had forgotten how the strange tilt of his light-blue eyes gave his face a look of lazy sensuality. She turned to flee back into her dreams, but they would not let her in.

There was a long silence.

Giles studied Susie's bent head. He wanted to hurt her, to make her look fully at him, to be aware of him. He decided the only way to do that was to spite her by getting married. He had also better go very carefully, just in case another accidental death should happen at Blackhall Castle!

The days leading up to the ball passed very quickly indeed, the inhabitants being secure and happily tucked away from the gossip of London society.

It quickly got about the fashionable drawing rooms that Giles, Earl of Blackhall, was looking for a wife. Anxious debutantes scanned the morning's post, looking for the coveted invitation. Matchmaking mamas desperately cultivated Blackhall relatives, only to find to their disappointment that the relatives did not wish to have anything to do with Blackhall Castle since the old earl had insulted them all into a fury many years ago. At last the guest list was out and members of London's prestigious clubs settled over their betting books to decide the favorite. Odds of seven to one were laid on Lady Sally Dukann, fourteen to one on Miss Cecily Winthrope, and twenty to one on Miss Harriet Blane-Tyre.

Susie's days passed in a bustle of activity. Extra linen, extra towels, extra everything had to be ordered, which she did with an unfashionable eye for a bargain, using the shops in the local town and thereby creating a lot of goodwill and saving herself a lot of money. Susie had naively instructed the shops to send the bills to her man of business, instead of turning them all over to Giles.

Giles was busy as well, commanding his squads of workmen to prodigious efforts. There were so many guests to be housed. The large bailey in the outer courtyard had already been modernized and turned into suites of guest rooms, and now additional rooms were made in the large gatehouse.

Susie carefully wrote out cards in neat copperplate, with each guest's name to be pinned to respective bedroom doors "so that they don't creep into the wrong bed by mistake," as Carter informed her grimly. But Susie did not know of country-house affairs, where the sprightly guests crept along the corridors at night, deliberately looking for every bedroom but the right one.

Flowers had to be arranged in all the rooms, and flowering plants and bushes had to be planted in the new flower beds, which cut their elegant way across a former tract of grazing land. Stands of trees had to be planted along the edge of an already existing lake, and lanterns had to be slung through the new trees and strung through the courtyards between the grim old walls.

In the middle of all this fuss and activity, Carter, who had become Susie's lady's maid, reminded her mistress that she ought to think about purchasing a ball gown, and since only the best would do, my lady would be advised to make a visit to London. Susie shrank from leaving the enclosed world of the castle, but she was young and feminine enough to want to look her best for Giles's ball.

That was how she found herself back in London one hot spring day with the grim Carter in attendance. Carter knew all the best dressmakers and advised her young mistress to put herself in the hands of the famous Madame Henrietta. Madame Henrietta, despite her name, was not French but a middle-aged German Jewess with a clever eye. She leapt at the chance of outfitting the beautiful widowed countess, particularly when Susie murmured in her dreamy way that she didn't care how much it cost.

So in the hot little salon in Conduit Street, Susie was treated to her first fashion show. She was very startled and amused to find that the models wore severe long black dresses when showing evening gowns or underwear. One particularly haughty mannequin looked quite ridiculous modeling a frivolous French corset over her black gown.

Madame Henrietta finally talked her into purchasing a gown of gold-colored peau de soie. It was daringly low at the front and very low at the back. The bodice was ornamented with an exquisite fall of fine black lace, and the full skirt of the dress was cut open above the hem to reveal a dashing black lace petticoat. Susie demurred. The gown looked very French and rather naughty. Ah, but the touches of black lace showed a delicacy, a reminder of milady's recent bereavements, cooed Madame Henrietta in her mock French accent. Carter gave a sour nod of approval. Carter had taken one of her dislikes to Giles and privately thought the combination of Susie and the dress would "knock that young man in the eye. Him and his wanting to get married."

Carter, like the rest of the servants,

thought that Giles should marry Susie. That way their smuggling activities would go undisturbed.

Carter then took Susie off to several other shops. It was a new London to Susie, a London she had never seen before. Expensive shops with soft lights and soft carpets, obsequious sales people, glorious clothes, and exotic scents, and all to be charged and taken away.

Susie's day was spoiled by a small twinge of guilt. She felt she really should go and pay a visit to her parents. But when it came down to it, she simply could not. She was anxious to get back to the familiar world of the castle.

She wondered what Giles was doing, and then wondered why she cared.

Giles was lying on the floor at the top of the gatehouse, sweating hard.

He had been leaning over the battlemented parapet to watch the workmen below when the seemingly solid stone had given way under the pressure of his fingers. He had fortunately thrown himself back and away from the gaping hole that had appeared as a large lump of masonry had hurtled to the ground below.

A footman came running breathlessly up

the stairs, two at a time. He helped Giles to his feet and dusted him down. "It's mercy you're all right, my lord," he cried, "Just to think, it could have happened to my lady. She was up here yesterday, looking over, and she wouldn't have had the wit to throw herself back."

*"But what if you die?"* Susie's childish voice resounded in his brain. Could she have arranged this accident? It was impossible and yet . . .

All of a sudden he decided to pay a call on Inspector Disher. The inspector was not to be found at the police station but working in his shirt-sleeves in his little patch of garden. The inspector's home was very like the cottage of Susie's dreams. It had a heavy thatched roof, and tangled honeysuckle hung over a trellis around the low doorway.

"My lord!" exclaimed the inspector, delighted and gratified. "If you'll just stop in, I'll get my Mary to make us a cup of tea."

"This is not a social call," said Giles grimly.

The inspector gave him a quick look and then said, "Well, whatever it is, my lord, a cup of tea will come welcome on this hot day. Did you ever see the like, my lord? Downright un-English this weather is."

"I'm sorry to bother you on your day off," remarked Giles, bending his head and entering a pretty little parlor, where the policeman's wife stood bobbing and blushing. "Nice place you've got here."

"We do our best," said the inspector. "Now, Mary, run along to the kitchen and make his lordship a pot of tea, and bring some nice hot scones and some of your strawberry jam."

When his wife had gone, he adopted his official voice and manner. "Well, now, my lord, what can I do for you?"

The inspector settled his plump figure in a rocker and prepared himself to listen to some tale of poaching.

"It's about Lady Felicity's death," said Giles abruptly. "Are you quite sure it was an accident?"

The inspector straightened up slowly and stared at his noble guest in surprise. "I'm sure as sure, my lord. Of course, it was just a token investigation, you might say. Riding accidents are very common, and that there horse was a regular devil."

"Is," corrected Giles gently. "Is, Inspector. Lady Susie refused to have the beast shot."

"Did she now? Some ladies, of course, are very sentimental about animals. But let's get this straight, my lord. Can it be you suspect foul play?"

Giles smiled reluctantly. "I never knew policemen actually said that, but, yes, I am suspicious. First there was the accidental death of my uncle. Look, I'd better tell you the truth. The night of my uncle's death, Susie was standing at an upstairs window, looking out at the sea and saying aloud that she wished him dead. Shortly before Felicity died, the servants say that Susie shouted at her in the dining room and said she wished her dead. Recently Lady Susie was talking about her son inheriting the castle. I pointed out that I am the heir, and she said, 'Oh! But what if you die?' " Giles went on to tell the inspector about his accident of the afternoon.

"Therefore," he ended, "I decided that there were too many coincidences, too many accidents. I decided it might do no harm to reopen an investigation into Lady Felicity's death."

"Do you want an official investigation?" asked the inspector.

"No," said Giles slowly. "I wondered if you could take up the case in your spare time. Go over the ground again. Talk to my head groom. I'll tell him to be discreet. Find out if there was anyone in the vicinity, a tramp or a shepherd or a child. I'll pay you well."

The inspector rubbed his forehead in a puzzled way. "I don't mind saying, a bit of extra money would come in handy, my lord, and I've got a bit of leave due to me. But I've a feeling Lady Blackhall is innocent. You now tell me you heard her saying she wanted her husband dead — which you really ought to have told me at the time, you know. But I can tell you this, my lord. That accident to the old earl happened the way she said it did. Couldn't be any other way. How could a slip of a thing like Lady Susie push a great, hulking man like the earl out of the window?"

"She must be stronger than she looks," said Giles stubbornly. "She's the only person who's ever been able to master that brute Dobbin." Now that he had started, Giles was strangely determined to find Susie guilty.

"Very well, my lord," said Inspector Disher. "But don't be disappointed if I don't find out anything. You'd better take that foreman, Sam Cobbett, up to the gatehouse and get him to examine the masonry. If anyone's been tampering with it, he'll know. Ah, here's Mary with tea. Try one of these scones, my lord."

Giles left as soon as he politely could. As soon as he returned to the castle, he took Sam Cobbett up to the roof of the gatehouse. "I've already seen it, me lord," grumbled Sam, "and it's only that there bit that was weak. The rest's as strong as anything."

"Had it been weakened deliberately?" asked Giles.

"Oh, no," said Sam in surprise. "Reckon a cannon ball or rocks or somethink hit that bit back in the old days, like. See here. It's all crumbled and broke. My men'll have it fixed in a trice. I've got the best bricklayer in Essex down there."

Giles went thoughtfully back to the keep. He now felt a bit of a fool for having set the inspector to investigate Lady Felicity's death. But there was, after all, something rather strange about Susie. He would study her more closely in the days to come.

But Giles had little time to study Susie, for the very next day the first of the house guests began to arrive.

The three hopeful debutantes were rather taken aback to find a very pretty young widow already in residence in the castle. Jealousy made them treat Susie very badly. Susie was locked away in her dreams and hardly noticed, but Giles did and obscurely blamed Susie for lowering his three hopeful candidates in his eyes. All the guest rooms in the keep, the bailey, and the gatehouse were soon full, and Giles found another thorn sticking in his flesh. He had invited several of his bachelor friends down for the ball, and every one of them seemed to be trailing around after Susie, with their tongues hanging out. They openly envied him for having such a lovely girl right under his nose, so to speak.

The elder guests, the ones without marriageable daughters, that is, all obviously found Susie charming and congratulated Giles on having such a delightful chatelaine.

The servants had all but forgotten their suspicions and fears of Susie until the head groom, Clifton, dropped his bombshell. The inspector had asked him some very searching questions about the day of Lady Felicity's death and had said that he was looking for a witness. The inspector had sworn Mr. Clifton to secrecy, and Mr. Clifton had told no one but his friend the housekeeper, Mrs. Wight. Mrs. Wight had confided this tantalizing piece of gossip to Thomson over a bottle of the best smuggled port, and Thomson, feeling the secret too heavy to bear, had drunk more than was good for him and had confided in Henry, the footman, who was engaged to one of the upstairs maids, and Henry told *her*. And so it went on until the whole servants' hall seethed with gossip.

"Master Giles'll be the next to go," they said gloomily. Hadn't Lady Susie said he might die?

Unaware of all this activity, Susie competently handled the management of the large household and enjoyed the novelty of being courted by several dashing young men all at the same time.

But it was one late arrival who almost made her heart stop. Here was the pleasant, homely young man of her dreams! He was not a friend of Giles's but turned out to be Miss Cecily Winthrope's brother, Arthur. Arthur had never had any success with the ladies, being accounted a prize bore by both sexes. But his sister, Cecily, was quick to notice Susie's interest and went all out to encourage her brother. Susie was a very wealthy widow, she pointed out. And with Susie out of the way, she, Cecily, could have a clear field with Giles, for although Giles pretended not to be interested in the young countess, Cecily's eyes, sharpened by jealousy, had noticed that Giles watched Susie more than was necessary.

The handsome young bachelors were amazed and then angry to find the pretty Susie quite happy to spend her free time in the boring Arthur Winthrope's company and gloomily turned their attentions elsewhere.

Susie was obviously enchanted with Arthur. All his conversational grunts and monosyllables she put down to manly reticence, and in her dreamy innocence she did not notice the rather nasty wet gleam that was beginning to appear in his eyes, or the way his eyes were roving freely over her body.

Giles became violently jealous of Arthur. But Giles did not know he was jealous. He merely thought Susie was a dangerous, scheming murderess, and he wanted to do all sorts of nasty things to her, like crushing her in his arms and forcing a confession from her.

Arthur meant to propose to Susie on the night of the ball and, had he waited until then, she would have certainly accepted him.

But he did not.

Susie, convinced that they were soul mates, decided to take Arthur to her favorite spot down below the bluebell wood, which she had shown to no one else. While Arthur plodded stolidly beside her in his natty blazer and white flannels and straw boater, Susie had a long conversation with him in her mind.

"This is my favorite place, darling," she said to the dream Arthur.

"Gosh, it's pesky hot," said the real Arthur. "Where is this place?"

"Not far," said Susie, smiling, and went back to the dream Arthur, who was saying, "It's beautiful, absolutely beautiful. Those bluebells are the color of your eyes."

"Silly," teased dream Susie. "My eyes are brown."

"You expect me to go down there?" complained the real Arthur as they stood at last on top of the small cliff above the bluebell wood. "My trousers will be ruined."

"We can go down by that little gully," said Susie. "Come along. We shall be quite alone. Just the two of us."

"I say," said Arthur, turning brick-red with lust and excitement. "I say, by Jove, eh what."

He followed her gleefully down the slope, staring eagerly about him to make sure the spot was as secluded as Susie had told him.

Susie sat down on the boulder with a sigh of satisfaction. "Come and sit by me, darling," she thought she said to the dream Arthur, but she said it out loud.

"By Jove, yes, what, eh," said Arthur, plumping himself eagerly beside her. "Hot stuff, what?"

Susie's dream was rudely shattered as Arthur seized her in a surprisingly strong grip, forced her mouth up to his, and shoved a hot, wet tongue between her lips. Having effectively gagged her, he clamped a leg over her body and began to rock himself up and down, making nasty noises in the back of his throat.

Giles had been right about one thing: Susie *was* stronger than she looked, and she was driven nearly mad with fear and disgust. She gave one terror-inspired heave and thrust, and tongue and legs and groping hands all suddenly disappeared in a loud splash as Arthur went hurtling back into the water.

His straw hat bobbed away on the waves, and his greased head popped above the water. "Help!" he cried. "I can't swim!"

He was very near the boulder, which was covered by stringy seaweed at its base. He grabbed hold of it and tried to pull himself out of the water. Susie turned to flee. Her boot slipped on a patch of slime and she accidentally stamped on Arthur's hand. He gave a cry and went under again.

"Are you trying to kill him?" demanded an icy voice behind Susie's left shoulder, and she screamed in fright. Giles was standing behind her. He had been walking along the top of the cliff, looking for her, because he had heard from Lady Matilda that Susie had gone off walking with Arthur without a chaperon. He had been sure he would find her at her favorite place, and he was right. He had been annoyed and sickened to find the couple at the foot of the cliff clutched in what looked like an extremely torrid embrace and had been about to turn away when he had suddenly seen Susie throw Arthur into the water. Now, as he hurried down the hill, it looked to him as if she had deliberately stamped on Arthur's hand as he was trying to climb out.

He stretched down and jerked Arthur out of the water. Arthur lay in the prickly grass beside the boulder and gasped like a landed cod.

Giles expected Arthur to accuse Susie of murder, but to his surprise it was Susie who began the accusations. "How dare you?" she shouted down at the gasping Arthur. "How dare you maul me and touch me?"

Arthur found his breath and sat up wrathfully. "Well, what do you expect?" he cried. "Listen, Giles. She says to me, she's going to take me to a place where we can be all alone. What was I to think, eh? I ask you, as a man of the world, what was I to think? So I try to kiss her, and she pushes me in the drink. I mean, she's a *married* woman —"

"Go back to the castle and get changed, Arthur," said Giles quietly. "I'll escort Lady Susie home." His sympathies had abruptly switched to Susie. Arthur was a repulsive, caddish beast.

Arthur stood up and gave the couple a slow grin. "So it's like that, is it?" He leered. "Well, well, well. By Jove, eh what? *What?*" The last "what" was because Giles had kicked him in the seat of the pants as he had turned around. "Pack your bags when you get back, Arthur," said Giles sweetly, "or I'll drown you personally."

Arthur took one look at Giles's cold blue eyes and scrambled up the slope with the agility of a mountain goat.

Giles turned a look at Susie. Either she was a consummate actress, or she had indeed had a bad shock. Her face was white, and her eyes for the first time since the death of her husband had a wide-awake, *alive* stare, as if she had newly found herself in this present world of reality and didn't like it one bit.

"Is it always going to be like that?" she sobbed wildly. "Messy and hot and groping? Oh, it makes me sick. It's not what I'd dreamed it would be. Not at all."

Giles led her gently up the slope while all the time she cried bitterly. At last, when they reached the top of the cliff, he spread his jacket on the grass and urged her to sit down and compose herself before returning to the castle. He handed her a large pocket handkerchief to dry her tears and then settled back to wait for her to recover. He stared at the slim shoulders, bent in front of him, shaking with sobs, and he longed to put his arms around her and comfort her, but he had not yet made up his mind. No human being could cause so many accidents, if accidents they were. A long strand of hair had escaped from its moorings and hung down over the high-boned collar of her blouse. He absent-mindedly reached out and picked it up, watching the sun glint through its silky threads.

The sun was scorching his back, and he

impatiently loosened his collar stud, took off his collar and his tie, and threw them on the grass. He opened the neck of his shirt, feeling the cool breeze against the two inches of naked skin at his throat. Then he realized that Susie had stopped crying and was staring at his state of undress with shock and dismay.

"Don't look so shocked," he teased her gently. "You have seen me in my bathrobe and pajamas, you know." This was true, as they shared the one and only bathroom at the top of the keep.

"But you look more dressed in your bathrobe," said Susie timidly, gazing fascinatedly at the faint gold hairs curling above the edge of his shirt. She wondered how far the hairs went and blushed painfully.

All Giles's suspicions of her fled. No actress could have conjured up that blush. He felt a sudden wave of protective tenderness for her. He felt like the veriest cad. As soon as he got back to the castle, he would use the newly installed telephone and call off Inspector Disher.

The air was heavy with the hot smells of the late spring countryside. Lazy bees bumbled through a clump of bramble flowers nearby, and the sea hissed and whispered at the foot of the cliff. Over the rise, and standing proudly above its gray walls in the dazzling sunlight, stood Blackhall Castle, with its standard flying bravely from the top of the keep. Giles felt suddenly exhilarated and happy.

He reached forward and took her hand gently in his while she sat with her head turned a little away from him, the sun and the wind playing in the floating tendrils of her hair. She let her hand lie passively in his, held prisoner by the strange current of emotion that seemed to be passing between them.

A sea gull sailed lazily overhead, glaringly white against the pale-blue sky. The breeze sent a blue wave rippling through the bluebells down to the water.

There was an apologetic cough from behind them, and both started and turned around. Giles began to laugh. A large jersey cow stood staring down at them like an outraged dowager. He reluctantly helped Susie to her feet. "Let's go back," he said. "It's nearly teatime. Arthur will have left by now, and we had better attend to our guests."

Dazed by the sun and the heat and the mixture of strange emotions in her body, Susie walked a little away from him, and they made their way side by side toward the castle. So strong was the electric emotion between them, they could have been wrapped in one another's arms.

To the guests seated around the dinner table that evening, there was no doubt about the name of Giles's future bride. They did not sit together. They hardly exchanged a word; but there was something in the atmosphere between Susie and Giles that fairly charged the air. Miss Cecily Winthrope privately and viciously blamed her brother, who had played his cards so badly. Harriet Blane-Tyre, a jolly Scotch redhead, gave a mental shrug and turned her roving eye to one of the other available bachelors. Lady Sally Dukann sat and openly sulked.

Giles was so immersed in his new feelings of warmth and tenderness toward Susie that he forgot to telephone the inspector. Susie let herself become absorbed in this new and very real enchantment and forgot to dream.

Lady Matilda, who was as sharp as her needles, smiled at both benignly and dropped a great variety of magenta stitches.

But not one person in the elegant dining room, with its newly enlarged table and its pretty paintings, could ever begin to imagine on this beautiful evening just what a terrible disaster Giles's ball was going to prove to be.

# Chapter Seven

The day of the ball dawned beautiful, clear, and sunny, with that same light breeze drifting in from the sea.

Carriages rattled to and from the station all day, bringing the remainder of the guests. Maids rushed between the rooms, carrying armfuls of silks and laces. The orchestra was already rehearsing in a large striped marquee in the courtyard, and in another marquee against the other wall, servants were setting up long buffet tables and an improvised bar.

Susie had hired such a generous contingent of extra staff that the servants of the castle felt that they might perhaps be able to enjoy some of the festivities as well. Outside the castle walls, huge stands were being erected for a firework display. Giles meant to throw the party of the season.

At one point in the afternoon, he went in search of Susie and found her at last with an ink stain on her nose, bent over the housekeeping ledgers.

"Leave all that," he said gaily, "and let's

go for a walk. You've got an ink blot on your pretty little nose. Go and take it off first."

Susie gave him a radiant smile and slammed the books shut. In a trice she had changed into a pretty, cool linen skirt and cotton blouse and had scrubbed her face and was running back down the stairs to join him.

They strolled away from the castle through the brand-new gardens and down to the edge of the lake. Susie unfurled her lace parasol and strolled along by the water's edge with Giles, feeling as if she were moving in the sunny landscape of a dream.

"You never really told me how you came to marry my uncle," said Giles. "Do you feel you could tell me now?"

Susie did. She explained about her parents' ambitions, and how they had threatened to turn her out in the street if she did not obey them. For the first time she began to describe her fear of the old earl and of his coarse manners.

"Is love always like that?" she asked shyly. "Always so brutal? First your uncle, and then Arthur."

"No," said Giles, catching hold of her hand and pulling her down to sit beside him on a stone bench. "It is something very rare and precious. I'm only beginning to realize it now. I thought I loved my wife, but now I realize I did not know the meaning of the word. I was angry when I divorced her; angry because she had left me for someone else. But it's been a long time since I've even thought of her.

"Poor Susie. I thought you were a wicked, scheming girl. How can you forgive me?"

"Easily," said Susie with an enchanting laugh, looking up at him from under the shadow of her straw hat.

It flashed through Giles's mind that he had not yet called off the inspector, but her mouth was now turned up toward his, soft and inviting.

He kissed her very tenderly and chastely on the lips, not wanting to frighten her at this early stage with an excessive show of passion. Susie kissed him gently back. For the present, they were both happy to exchange soft, lingering kisses as the sun sparkled on the water and the swallows swooped and dived over their busy reflections. Giles sat bareheaded, his hand resting lightly on Susie's waist, feeling her heart beat through the heavy armor of stays. There was very little of Susie left bare to kiss, apart from her face. A high-boned collar covered her neck, and long leg-of-mutton sleeves covered her arms. She wore a little pair of white kid gloves fastened with pearl buttons. Her linen skirt was very long and only showed the long points of her openwork shoes.

He slowly unfastened the little buttons at the wrist of her glove and then turned the leather back to expose her white wrist, with its delicate network of pale-blue veins.

He bent his head and kissed her there, pressing his lips harder against the tiny throbbing veins and then moving his tongue gently against the skin. Susie began to shiver. She wanted him to do more. She wanted him to stop. She could not bear the churning turmoil of her feelings.

Passion reared its good old ugly head, and the peace of the afternoon was broken. Susie did not understand these strange fluttering pains in the pit of her stomach, and Giles was frightened of scaring her. He quietly buttoned up her glove and, smiling down at her tenderly, he kissed her gently on the nose.

"Let's get back, poppet," he said. "I might forget myself, and after all, we have all the time in the world."

"We must talk more," said Susie with a feeling of apprehension. "You do not really know me. I don't know much about you."

"Tonight," he said. "Spare me as many dances as you can."

"But people will talk if I dance with you more than once!" protested Susie.

"Let them talk!" he cried, catching hold of her by the waist and swinging her around. "Everyone must be able to see I'm in love with you."

"Oh, Giles," cried Susie, her eyes misting over with happy tears. "Did you say you loved me?"

But Giles's attention had been caught by a small party of men who were heading toward the castle gate. "The Customs men," he said with surprise. "I wonder what they want? Maybe they think the castle's a smugglers' hideout." He threw back his head and laughed. But when he had finished laughing at his own joke, he was to find that Susie had gone.

"Susie!" he called out in surprise and set out after her at a run, amazed at how swiftly the girl could move. Her white skirt flickered over the drawbridge and under the portcullis. As the Customs men approached over the drawbridge the portcullis fell with a tremendous crash, making them jump back in alarm.

They turned and looked at Giles in

amazement as he came running up. "Sorry about that," gasped Giles. "Faulty machinery."

But in his heart he knew that Susie had operated the lever on the other side to lower the portcullis and so keep the excisemen out — and he wondered why.

"Someone will be along to open it in a minute," he said, turning to the leader of the party. "Meanwhile, what's all this about?"

"Smuggling wine and brandy, my lord," said the chief officer, who introduced himself as Mr. Pottifer. "There's been French fishing boats seen lying off below the castle at night. Just a routine check of your cellars, my lord."

"Of course," said Giles mechanically while his mind raced. "Hey you!" he called to Henry, the footman, who was hurrying across the courtyard on the other side of the portcullis. "Hurry and open this thing up."

Henry walked toward the portcullis with very slow, stately steps, and Giles watched him with growing suspicion. The servants were so well trained, he was used to their jumping to his bidding. Something was wrong, and Susie knew about that something. Oh, God, not another woman who was other than she seemed! All his darkest suspicions about Susie came tumbling back.

At last the portcullis creaked reluctantly upward. Giles and the Customs men hurried through. He took them straight to the cellars. The door was standing open, and the bland figure of Thomson was just emerging with a couple of bottles of champagne in his hand. "Just taking some extra up to put on ice, my lord," he said and then gave a start that Giles thought was decidedly theatrical. "Why, who are these gentlemen, my lord?"

"As you can see, these are excisemen, Thomson," snapped Giles. "Stand aside and let them examine the cellars."

Thomson gave his master a hurt look and then stepped out into the hall. Mr. Pottifer hurried down the stone steps of the cellar and Giles followed.

At last Mr. Pottifer looked up from his inspection of a rack of claret. "I owe you an apology, my lord," he said heavily. "Everything's in order here."

"Did you actually suspect me of smuggling?" demanded Giles.

"Oh, not you, my lord," said Mr. Pottifer. "But there's a lot of butlers around this part of the coast who don't mind lining their own pockets by buying up a shipload of contraband and entering it in the books as an order from the wine merchant."

"I am sure Thomson would do no such thing," said Giles hotly. "He's been with the family for years."

"We were only doing our job," said Mr. Pottifer. "Best be on our way. We'd better look in at Lord Humfry's place farther along. There's been strange goings-on along this coast."

Giles followed the men up the cellar steps and then turned for a last look around. Something white gleamed in the darkness, caught at the back of one of the racks. He waited until Mr. Pottifer and his men had left and went slowly back down the cellar steps. He crossed to the rack, bent down and stretched his hand in, and tugged at a piece of white material. It was a small, lacy lady's handkerchief. He held it to his nose. It smelled faintly of Paradis, a scent that Susie usually wore.

He sat down on a barrel and thought hard. Susie dealt with the management of the household. She had control of her books. She had run like a startled hare when he had mentioned smuggling, and the next thing, the portcullis had conveniently dropped. So if anyone was behind smuggling, if anyone was feathering his or her own nest by fixing the books, it must be Susie.

*The scheming little bitch!* he thought furiously. *My uncle's fortune was not enough for her. Little gold digger. I was going to marry her. I said I loved her. Of course she wants to marry me. She wants her hands on my fortune so that any brat she might produce will take all this away from me.*

He searched the keep from top to bottom but there was no sign of Susie. He had not thought to look in the kitchens.

Susie was sitting at the kitchen table, surrounded by a bevy of anxious servants. "You see, my lady," Thomson was explaining, "the old earl knew what we was up to, and he didn't mind 'cause he liked the best of everything and didn't much care how it was come by. Then the wages haven't been changed around here for nigh on twenty years, but we none of us complained on account of the fact that we could make a bit out of the contraband by selling stuff to the houses around here. We'll need to lay off for a bit now, of course, but thanks to you, there's no harm done. But you must not tell my lord, for he'd be so mad, he'd fire the lot of us."

Susie looked at the circle of faces and bit her lip. She had a strong streak of loyalty in her, and she could not forget the servants' kindness to her.

She took a deep breath. "All right," she said. "I won't tell Giles anything. How did you manage to get everything away in time?"

"We hadn't much, my lady. The excisemen have been patrolling the cliffs this past fortnight. We had to buy all the stocks for the ball in the regular way. It took us no time at all to hide the rest down that back stairway."

"Very well," said Susie heavily. She tried to smile. "Don't all look so worried. I've said I won't tell Giles."

"It's not that, my lady," said Mrs. Wight, the housekeeper. "There's something we think you ought to know."

"What?" Susie looked up, amazed at the ring of concerned faces.

"You tell my lady, Thomson," said Mrs. Wight. "My nerves are that unstrung, I can't take any more. I always had the artistical temperament, and it always do give me wind round the heart."

Thomson looked slowly around at the other servants, who all nodded.

He pulled up a chair and sat down at the

146

table opposite Susie. He had not asked for permission to sit down, and that alone should have warned Susie that what he was about to impart was serious.

"It's like this, my lady. There's something about Lord Giles we think you ought to know. He suspects you of murdering Lady Felicity."

"No! I won't believe it!" cried Susie.

"It's true, my lady. He's hired that there Inspector Disher to investigate the case, private-like. Disher's already been snooping round the stables, questioning Clifton."

Susie looked pathetically around the ring of watching faces. They all nodded.

So her romance with Giles had been nothing more than another dream. She sat very still, very white, and very tense.

"Miss Carter," said Thomson to the lady's maid, "you'd best take your mistress upstairs and see she has a lie down."

Carter bustled forward, and Susie allowed herself to be led away.

Such a short time ago she had felt she was walking in a dream. Now she felt she was wandering through a black nightmare from which there was no awakening.

Giles was not able to find Susie until the ball had started. His attention had been claimed by the needs of his various guests. Now he stood on the edge of the ballroom floor and watched with cold blue eyes as Susie entered on the arm of Lady Matilda. She looked like an exquisite French painting, the combination of her seeming innocence and the daring sophistication of the dress making everyone turn and stare. Her eyes looked enormous in her white face, the gold of her dress bringing out sunny gold highlights in her sun-bleached brown hair. She wore a headdress of gold silk roses and carried a large black ostrich-feather fan. She no longer moved with the awkward, immature grace of a young colt but with the assured movements of a sophisticated woman.

She glanced fleetingly in his direction and then looked quickly away. He felt black anger beginning to boil up inside him, for that one look had carried a tinge of guilt, and that double-damned her in his eyes. He would not ask her to dance. He was determined not to make a scene in front of his guests. He had not reckoned on the presence of one Harry Carruthers, an old army friend. Harry was a perpetual bachelor who, nonetheless, adored pretty women. He was an entertaining rattle with a fund of witty and amusing stories. Like the old campaigner he was, he quickly routed the opposition and claimed Susie for the first dance.

At first Susie moved like a mechanical doll in his arms through the steps of the waltz, but then, over his broad shoulder, she saw Harriet Blane-Tyre clasped in Giles's arms, and a wave of hot jealousy washed over her. She began to laugh at all Harry's remarks, spurring that gallant fellow to further humorous efforts, and the blacker Giles's looks became, the more Susie laughed and laughed.

Still, he would not have created any public scene had he not been called to the newly installed telephone. Inspector Disher's voice bellowed from the other end of the line. Inspector Disher did not really believe in the telephone and felt he had to make his voice carry all the way to the castle by sheer volume.

"Don't shout," said Giles crossly, holding the heavy earpiece away from his ear. "What was that you said?"

"I said I've found a witness to Lady Felicity's death, my lord. It's a bad, bad business. Shocking!"

Giles gently placed the phone back on its table and backed away from it as the inspector's now tinny and indistinguishable voice crackled on. So it had been murder after all. He did not want to hear the details. As the inspector roared on about the bad business being Lady Felicity's shocking treatment of the horse, he marched back out into the courtyard and into the ballroom.

Susie saw him before he saw her, so that when he noticed her floating past in the arms of Harry Carruthers — again! — she was smiling languishingly up at that gentleman.

Giles hated her with an all-consuming passion.

He wanted revenge.

Now!

He marched up to the rostrum, where the band was playing, and held up his hand for silence.

The band fell silent. The guests stopped dancing. All faces turned in his direction.

He looked an awe-inspiring figure with his strangely tilted eyes blazing like twin chips of blue ice and his handsome face as white as the dazzling frill of his evening shirt.

"That woman," he said in a cold, carrying voice that dripped venom, "is a murderess!"

Everyone turned slowly and stared at

Susie, moving away slightly so that the dancers formed a long corridor down which Giles and Susie stared at each other.

"That was Inspector Disher on the telephone," Giles went on, never taking his eyes from Susie's face. "*Lady* Blackhall, my *dear* Susie, murdered Lady Felicity."

Several hundred breaths drew in in a hiss of shock. "Not only that, but this Lady Macbeth here has been using my home to feather her nest. She has been using this castle as a center for her smuggling activities. My late uncle's fortune was not enough for her, you see, and in the light of this latest news, I wonder if she came by it honestly. You, Henry, and that other footman, take her away and lock her in her rooms until the police arrive!"

Giles gave a signal to the band, which immediately started to play. Susie was led from the room by the two men, and not even Harry Carruthers moved to stop them.

The ball was a disaster after that. Several of the ladies felt obliged to faint to prove their delicate sensibilities, and most of the gentlemen found it a good excuse to get drunk.

Giles's rage and misery seemed to permeate the whole castle. Married couples began to squabble openly, and the elderly Earl of Murr could be heard calling his wife a "frozen-faced old muffin."

The braver of the debutantes tried to resume their flirtations, but there were not many gentlemen to flirt with, since they were mostly across the courtyard in the bar, discussing the delicious scandal and making large inroads into the stock of iced champagne.

Giles waited miserably and drearily for the law to arrive. He waited. And waited.

At last he telephoned the police station, only to be told that — as he might have guessed — Inspector Disher was on leave and was not on the telephone at home. Nonetheless, Giles was surprised that the inspector had not called in at his station to collect a constable to assist him in his arrest. Perhaps he thought Giles was paying him to hush the whole thing up. Well, he was bloody well mistaken, thought Giles savagely. He would see Susie dangling on the end of a rope at Newgate if it was the last thing he did, and that would teach her to flirt with Harry Carruthers! With that latest insane thought, Giles realized that he was mad with jealousy. A cold hand of doubt clutched at his heart. What exactly had the inspector said? He had said it was a bad business. That was all. Oh, God!

Giles sent a postillion to the inspector s cottage, demanding that gentleman's presence at the castle immediately. But the inspector chose to arrive in person only some ten minutes later.

Giles ushered the inspector into the library of the keep while the laughing, dancing, tinny music of the faraway band seemed to mock him.

Inspector Disher was perspiring freely, having walked and half run all the way on foot. He removed his bowler, which left an angry red rim around his worried forehead, and said, "I couldn't wait till the morning, my lord. Why didn't you listen to me?"

"I'm sorry," said Giles dully. "Tell me about it."

The inspector produced a large notebook, opened it up, and cleared his throat. "A certain young lad called Freddie Winkler was brought to my attention. He's a lad of about nine, and he's always playing round the old gravel pit, though Mrs. Winkler has said she'll tan his hide if she catches him there again. Well, it so happens that that there lad was round the gravel pit on the day of Lady Felicity's accident."

"And?"

"And he says like it was a shocking business, and he hadn't told nobody 'cause he was frightened, and furthermore his ma would whip him if she found out he'd been playing there."

"Get to the point, man," said Giles tersely. "What did this child see?"

"He was up near the top of the pit," said the inspector, "and he sees Lady Felicity behaving in a shocking way. The child says she was half murdering that horse, Dobbin, cutting at him with her whip till the beast bled, sawing at his mouth, and a-digging with her spur. It's a bad business — cruelty to animals. Were her ladyship alive, I'd have her in court for cruelty, lady or no lady."

"So the horse threw her?"

"Yes, my lord. It all happened just the way Lady Susie said it did."

Giles felt sick.

He'd done it again.

But worse was to come.

After the gratified inspector had left with a sizable check in his jacket pocket, Giles was about to leave the study when he found himself confronted by the stately person of his butler and the round figure of his housekeeper, both asking to have a word in private with him.

He walked back into the study and motioned them to sit down.

"I'd prefer to stand, my lord," said Thomson anxiously, "for you're not going to like what you're going to hear."

"I'll be the judge of that, Thomson."

"Very well, my lord, but we'd rather stand. It's about the smuggling."

"Go on."

"It was nothing really to do with my lady, my lord. We started the contraband business away back in the old earl's day, during his second marriage. See, like we told Lady Blackhall, our wages have remained the same for the past twenty years, and the old earl, he preferred to let us make a bit at smuggling rather than pay us any more. Now, Lady Susie, she found out by accident. She seemed to think it was a bit of a game. She's just a romantic young girl, my lord.

"But she saved our necks when the excisemen came calling, and we pleaded with her to say nothing to you. But we couldn't none of us stand by and let her take the blame."

Giles sat as if turned to stone.

"And if she did kill Lady Felicity," put in Mrs. Wight stoutly, "then good luck to her, for her ladyship treated my young lady something crool, that she did, always sneering and tormenting and worritting her."

"Lady Felicity's death was an accident," said Giles. "I discovered that this evening."

There was a long silence.

"I suppose," said Thomson, clearing his throat, "that you'll be wishing to call the authorities and have us turned over?"

"No," said Giles abruptly. "Good God, no! I have caused enough misery this evening. You will cease this trade, and all your wages will be reviewed and increased accordingly. Now, please go and leave me alone!"

Thomson and Mrs. Wight were only too grateful to escape and spread the glad news among the other servants.

Giles sat in the library for a long time. Then he went slowly back to the ballroom to make his second announcement of the evening.

"I must have been insane," he told his startled audience. "Lady Susie is guiltless. She is no murderess, nor yet a smuggler. I have made a ghastly mistake."

Harry Carruthers stepped smartly up to Giles and blacked his eye, and Giles socked him on the mouth. Various drunken young men decided to settle old scores there and then. The Countess of Murr tottered into the buffet, picked up a large blancmange, and emptied it over her husband's gray head, shouting, "Who's a frozen-faced old muffin now, you old goat?"

Harriet Blane-Tyre, overcome with champagne and excitement, allowed herself to be led off to a dark spot of the grounds and seduced by a very unfashionable and almost penniless young man. Cecily Winthrope threw her arms around the second fiddle and told him she loved him madly. Over in the buffet, the Earl of Murr retaliated by tipping jelly down his wife's august cleavage, cheered on by a group of wild young men who all seemed to have black eyes, bleeding noses, and torn shirt frills.

Giles fled from the scene as soon as he could and ran to the top of the keep.

Susie's bedroom and sitting-room doors were wide open. A glance was enough to assure him that all her clothes were gone. A faint aroma of Paradis hung in the still, empty room to mock his folly, and down below, the best of England's aristocracy crunched among the broken glass, threw cakes and lobster patties at each other, and had a perfectly splendid time.

Under a full moon, Lady Matilda's antique carriage lumbered on its way to London with the indefatigable Lady Matilda knitting in one corner and Susie, dry-eyed and white-faced, in the other.

On the opposite seat sat a grim and disapproving Carter. They were bound for Susie's parents' home in Camberwell, and Carter did not like that one bit.

Behind the carriage trotted an evil-looking horse called Dobbin. Every time the carriage stopped, he tried to stave in the back of it with his hooves just to pass the time, but the occupants of the carriage were too wrapped up in their own thoughts to care whether he succeeded.

Susie sat in a dry ache of physical and mental misery. Nothing had hurt her so badly before, neither the death of her husband nor the death of Lady Felicity. This time she felt she was mourning her own death; the death of all that was young and romantic and free and tender and fresh.

She sat in numb misery as the miles slipped by and the sky grew paler and paler, until an angry red sun rose above the horizon of the black Essex marshes.

But to those who live in fantasies, a special release from pain is granted, a release denied to the poor souls who have grown to maturity, left their childhood dreams behind, and stared reality straight in the eye.

Down in the black pit of Susie's abject misery, a little dream began to take root, grow, and blossom. By the time the weary horses had stopped at a large posthouse to allow the night travelers some much-needed rest, it was in full flower.

Lady Matilda had said roundly that Giles had been talking a lot of codswallop about murder and would come to his senses in the morning. But Susie decided that she would be arrested for murder and hauled off to Newgate Prison.

She would stand in the dock at the Old Bailey, with her head thrown back and her veil thrown back, and she would bravely outstare the accusing eyes of Giles across the courtroom. "Prisoner at the bar," said the judge (stab-stab-stab) — for the judge was none other than Basil Bryant — "How do you plead?"

"Not guilty," said Susie in a loud, clear voice, while across the court Giles gnashed his teeth in rage. The evidence would mount against her. A wicked smile would play across Giles's evil lips. At the last breathtaking moment a surprise witness — an old tramp or somebody like that — would be rushed in. He would have seen the whole thing. She would be acquitted. The bells would ring, and the people would cheer. Basil would severely reprimand Giles. FAMOUS PHILANDERER, GILES, EARL OF BLACKHALL, TRIES TO RUIN HEIRESS, the headlines would scream, and as he left the court the angry mob would tear him to pieces.

By the time Carter put Susie to bed at the inn, a gentle smile was playing across her mistress's lips, and Susie fell asleep with the roar of the London mob, crying for Giles's blood, sounding comfortably in her ears.

# Chapter Eight

The Camberwell visit was a disaster from almost the start. After Mrs. Burke had enjoyed all the neighbors staring at a real, live countess, she began to nourish a deep-seated resentment for Carter. Right at the start the lady's maid had said in chilly accents that it was not her place to do Mrs. Burke's hair or to help her dress. Mrs. Burke had said rather incoherently that an unwilling servant was like an adder nourished in one's bosom, to which Carter had replied with a disdainful sniff.

Lady Matilda was an added disappointment, in that she did not look like a lady with her trailing old-fashioned clothes and endless pieces of sewing and knitting. She had ensconced herself in the most comfortable armchair in the front parlor, from which she had refused to budge, and listened in to all Mrs. Burke's talks with her friends.

Dr. Burke had found his little girl changed into an elegant lady he did not know in the slightest. He too began to build up a resentment. With all her fortune, Susie had not supplied one penny to the household, and her mad entourage was costing him a small fortune. Her coachman and two footmen — or rather Lady Matilda's — had had to be supplied with accommodation at a nearby ale-house. The stabling and fodder for the horses all had to be paid for.

He had hinted, he had suggested, he had pleaded downright poverty, and his dreamy daughter had not appeared to have listened to one word he said.

In despair, he finally faced her with the problem outright. He called her into his study and, telling her to sit down, swung his swivel chair around from his desk to face her.

"My dear Susie," he began, stroking his beard. "You are my daughter."

"Yes," replied his daughter in a vague way.

"You must honor and obey your father and mother."

"Yes," said Susie, yawning.

"Your mother and I are very poor people, very poor indeed."

"Oh!"

"Listen, Susie," said her father, moving into the attack. "I cannot afford to go on paying for your guest and your servants."

"Why didn't you say so, Papa?" said Susie infuriatingly. "I shall give you money."

Dr. Burke visibly brightened. "How much?" he asked eagerly.

"Present me with the bills," said Susie, "and I will take them to Mr. Jasper, my man of business."

This practical approach did not suit the doctor at all. He wanted more than the mere payment of the household bills.

"Look, Susie," he said earnestly. "You are a very rich girl. Don't you think it unfair that your poor father should still have to work for a living?"

"I might have done," replied Susie fairly, "if you and Mama had not told me so many times that your work was God's business. Healing the sick and all that," she added helpfully.

Dr. Burke put a quaver in his voice. "I am a very old man Susie. . . ."

"You are younger than my late husband," put in Susie with a tinge of acid in her young voice.

Her father stared at her in exasperation. "Are you going to give me any money or not?" he demanded.

"Oh, yes," said Susie calmly. "I shall see

Mr. Jasper this very day."

"I shall come with you," said Dr. Burke, rubbing his hands gleefully. "You must leave these money matters to us men of the world."

"No," said Susie flatly. "I have discovered I am quite clever when it comes to handling money. The money is mine, Papa, and I feel I have earned it in ways you could never begin to imagine."

Dr. Burke turned an embarrassed color of puce. He thought she was hinting at unmentionable sexual matters, and so he let her escape. He did not know the earl had leapt to his death before anything interesting had happened.

Mr. Jasper was delighted to see Susie. He had invested her fortune wisely and told her with pride that it had almost doubled. He readily agreed to settle a large amount on Susie's parents, a gesture that gladdened his old-fashioned heart.

Then, settling back in his chair and carefully putting the tips of his fingers together, he asked Susie why she had left Blackhall Castle.

Susie told him, beginning calmly enough and ending up in a heavy and refreshing burst of tears. Mr. Jasper removed his pince-nez, sent a clerk to fetch tea, and patted Susie on the shoulder in a clumsy but reassuring way.

"It's a miracle nothing about this got into the newspapers," he said. "Has young Giles gone mad?"

"I don't know," wailed Susie. "I never want to see him again."

"And are you happy at Camberwell?"

Susie dried her tears and looked at him and then said slowly, "I don't think I am. Is it very terrible, Mr. Jasper, not to like one's own parents?"

"No, only very natural," said Mr. Jasper, smiling. "In time, as you grow older, you will learn to forgive them for their idiosyncracies. Ah, tea, the cup that cheers, as the poet says. Now, drink up, my lady, and tell me more of Camberwell itself. Is your parents' house *large* enough for all of you?"

"Not really," said Susie. "And does it sound very snobbish of me? — but it all seems so poky and dark."

"You are a young lady of fortune and title," said Mr. Jasper, hitching his chair closer. "You should be taking your place in society and going to all the balls and parties. Lady Matilda could chaperon you and, as a young widow, you would have much more freedom than, say, a debutante."

"But I don't know how to get into society," said Susie.

"You *are* in," said Mr. Jasper cynically. "You have a title, a fortune, and you're young and marriageable. All you need is to set up your establishment somewhere in the West End. Rent a place first, and then we will look around for something to buy. I could arrange everything for you, servants and all. It is my job, you know. I extract quite a large fee from your income, you know, but I like to earn it."

"Very well, then," said Susie, seeing a whole new world opening in front of her. Hope began to spring anew. She would go to balls and parties, and she would soon forget Giles, soon lose this terrifying lost, black ache inside her body.

Giles had easily discovered Susie's whereabouts from the servants. After all, he was about to raise their wages, so they were anxious to oblige him in every way they could. They reasoned that he was really in love with Susie and would probably marry her, so they weren't being disloyal to the girl who had saved them from the excisemen.

Instead of rushing to lay his apology at her feet, Giles sent a messenger with a brief note, expressing his apologies in stilted sentences, which sounded slightly offensive, as if he didn't care one way or the other. Susie, crying over it, did not know that she was reading the final draft of about fifty torn-up letters and hours of mental anguish.

Giles felt his first duty lay with his guests. His family honor was at stake. He had landed in this mess by allowing his feelings to rule his head. He had behaved disgracefully. His ball had been worse than an undergraduate rag.

His noble guests were soothed on the following day by extravagant presents, gold cigarette cases for the men and gold watches for the ladies, and by the news that the *real* ball was to take place that very evening.

It was, however, a restrained party of guests now assembled again in the ball-room under the striped marquee. Giles worked with a will. He danced with all the wallflowers; he kept as many men out of the bar as possible. The fireworks display, which had fortunately been overlooked in the drunken revels of the night before, was set alight to gasps of admiration from the party. The highlight of the evening's enter-tainment was a guest appearance of that celebrated opera star, Yvette Duval, whose soaring, perfect notes acted on the troubled souls of the guests like a blessing. Madame Duval had been rushed down by special train from London that very day and bribed with an enormous fee to perform, but Giles reflected it was worth every penny. The Earl of Murr hugged his wife and asked her in more gentle tones than she had ever heard him use before to forgive him.

Harriet Blane-Tyre took the bull by the horns and told the young man who had stolen her virginity that she would be obliged if he would forget about the whole silly thing, at which news he was much relieved, having parted with his own virginity in the process and not enjoyed a minute of it.

Lady Sally Dukann came out of her sulks and behaved almost prettily, and Cecily Winthrope chased Harry Carruthers with alarming zeal.

The evening was a resounding success, and all except Giles enjoyed themselves immensely.

Giles had come to the conclusion that he had not been in love with Susie at all. He had behaved disgracefully, of course, and could only hope she would in time forgive him, but he privately admitted to himself that he did not really want to see her again.

After all, she was middle-class. A girl of his own class, he felt sure, would not have made him lose his senses and behave in such a foolish and insane way.

In the days that followed, the guests left one after the other. At last there was only Giles left.

There was still modernization to oversee, electric light to be installed in the keep, and one of the guest bedrooms to be changed into a bathroom, so that he and Susie could have one each. Damn it! She wasn't coming back. What had made him think of that?

There were some fine rhododendrons from India to admire, and he had a lilac tree planted down by that stone bench at the lake. She might see it in flower if she were here next spring. . . . "What is up with me?" he asked himself.

He was having the boulders torn from that field by the gravel pit, so that wheat could be planted in the following year. He could almost see the wheat, turning and glinting in his mind's eye like the sun on Susie's hair. Damn the girl!

"She is not suitable," he told his mirror sternly. "Just think of her horrible encroaching parents. Think how she leaves a trail of death and disaster everywhere she goes. I am a handsome and rich young man. Women like me. I need a wife. I'm lonely, that's all."

But her ghost haunted the castle and its walks until one day, when he was inspecting the repairs to the top of the gatehouse, he saw the flutter of a white skirt away in the distance, at the top of the cliff by the bluebell wood. He ran and ran until he reached the top of the cliff and embarrassed one of the underhousemaids with one of his footmen, who were making sedate love in the bushes.

*I shall go to London when the summer is over and find myself a bride,* he decided, and, having made up his mind, he worked harder than ever to make the long days pass quickly.

Susie enjoyed the rest of the summer in her new residence in Hapsburg Row in Knightsbridge. It was a placid existence. Society had not yet heard of the manner of the deaths of the late earl or of Lady Felicity, and it now seemed as if they never would. But they knew that the young Countess of Blackhall was "common" — "greengrocer's daughter or something" —

and snubbed her accordingly.

Susie had come to expect just such behavior from her new peers and did not mind in the least. She spent pleasant sunny days wandering about the shops or exercising Dobbin in Hyde Park at the unfashionable hour.

Lady Matilda had explained her surprising championship of Susie by saying she thought she was a silly girl who needed an older woman to take care of her, and, with that, resumed her tangled knitting and sewing and appeared to forget Susie's very existence.

Lady Matilda, however, noticed more than anyone ever gave her credit for. She was very loyal to Giles and had judged him to be so much in love with Susie that he was behaving like a madman. She therefore considered it her duty to keep an eye on Susie and see that she did not get married to anyone else. She enjoyed Susie's unfashionable life, since she was left with plenty of time to tat and stitch and was not obliged to chaperon the girl anywhere at all.

Susie's new home was a large square white house built around the end of the last century. It had electric light in the reception rooms and gas in the bedrooms, and Susie considered it the height of modernity. A staff of servants had been hired for her by the efficient Mr. Jasper. All she really had to do was to check her housekeeping books, order new curtains and furniture, and keep a sharp lookout for the handsome young man she would marry.

Susie had decided that homely young men were not to be trusted — witness the appalling behavior of Arthur Winthrope. She conjured up a vision of a handsome young fellow who had a square tanned face, honest brown eyes, and brown wavy hair. He neither looked nor talked like Giles.

As Susie continued to be unaware of society, society began to feel a little piqued with the common countess. She should, they felt, have been running after them, seeking invitations, or riding in the Park at the fashionable hour, when they would have their rightful pleasure in cutting her dead. But she continued to go about her infuriating concerns completely unaware of any of them.

Then, one early autumn day in September, when the leaves in Hyde Park were just beginning to turn and there was a pleasurable nip in the smoky blue air, Susie got herself into a scrape that was to bring her to the notice of society and, for that matter, to the notice of the rest of Britain.

Susie was exercising Dobbin in the Park early that morning, when she was sure of having the Park practically to herself.

She was seated sidesaddle on Dobbin's back in a smart blue velvet riding habit, with a jaunty little topper perched on the top of her immaculately dressed brown hair. Dobbin was cantering sideways and rolling his eyes and tossing his head in a very frightening manner. Susie was undisturbed. She was used to clinging on for dear life and knew that Dobbin would settle down once he had asserted his independence.

But to two dowagers taking an early morning stroll, it was a shocking display of bad horsemanship. The ladies were the Honorable Miss Belinda Fforbes-Benedick and Lady Jessica Whyte, two formidable spinsters.

"Isn't that the Common Countess?" asked Miss Belinda of her companion.

Lady Jessica took out her lorgnette and glared through its lenses at the cavorting Dobbin with his pretty rider. "By gad, so 'tis," she exclaimed. "Can't handle a horse. Horrible-looking beast. Needs a touch of the crop. What's she doin'?"

"Feeding the brute sugar," said Miss Belinda, who had the sharper eyes.

"Well, if that don't beat all," said Lady Jessica, who was proud of her own horsemanship. "She ain't in Camberwell now, and so I shall tell her. Shouldn't be allowed out on that brute, since she can't handle it. I shall tell her for her own good."

Meanwhile Susie had leaned forward and given Dobbin a lump of sugar and patted his nose and talked soft nonsense in his ear, and the silly horse closed his eyes and stood still in a sort of ecstatic trance.

Lady Jessica marched up and stood under Dobbin's nose "Hey, you!" she said rudely to Susie.

Susie looked down in surprise. She did not wish to dismount, for without anything to use as a mounting block, she doubted whether she would be able to get back on Dobbin again. So she simply stayed where she was and said gently, "I am afraid I don't know your name. I believe we have not been introduced."

Susie meant to be polite, but to Lady Jessica it sounded like a colossal snub, and she turned a mottled puce with anger.

"Never mind that fiddle," she snapped. "You oughtn't to be allowed out on that beast. You're no horsewoman, miss! You're a disgrace. That animal needs a touch of the whip."

Somewhere in the back of Dobbin's small, narrow brain, alarm bells began to ring. That harsh, squawking voice reminded him of the cut of the whip and the stab of the spur. He stared down his long nose at Lady Jessica's hat. It was a black felt hat ornamented with a whole dead ptarmigan with red glass eyes. Dobbin decided he did not like Lady Jessica. Furthermore, he hated her hat.

He leaned forward and pulled Lady Jessica's hat from her head, dropped it on the grass, and then trampled on it with his great splay hooves.

Susie let out a little gasp of horror. Miss Belinda came waddling up to give her friend support.

"I'm really so very sorry . . ." began Susie, but Dobbin had decided to go home, and so he set off at a brisk canter with Susie hanging gamely on his back.

"You shall hear from my lawyers," screamed Lady Jessica. "Common little slut! Just you wait!"

Two days later Susie was summoned to appear at Marlborough Street Magistrates Court, charged with assault.

"Don't go," advised Lady Matilda calmly. "Send a lawyer instead."

"Who?" asked Susie.

"Don't know," said Lady Matilda. "Ask somebody."

And that is how Susie came to ask Basil Bryant, who had passed his bar exams the year before.

And that is how Basil Bryant came to be killed.

But when Susie initially saw Basil, he was as radiant as that young man could possibly be. He would not hear of her staying at home. This case would be a cause célèbre, he said, pacing Susie's elegant drawing room and stabbing his long bony finger in the air. He had shaved off his toothbrush mustache. His large nose gave him a commanding air, but his lank hair glittered with overmuch grease, and he had doused himself too liberally with eau de cologne.

Susie was horrified at the idea of going to court. She had no idea what it would be like, but her scared imagination conjured up a sort of Gilbert and Sullivan *Trial By Jury* scene, where everything and anything could happen.

The forthcoming trial received a great deal of publicity in the newspapers, since there wasn't much else to write about in that quiet month.

Giles read an account of Susie's forthcoming trial, swore, and ordered his man to pack his bags.

To Susie's eyes the court was refreshingly drab. She had to wait through a long series of charges for shoplifting and vagrancy before her name was called. The ladies, Belinda and Jessica, had elected to appear in court. So had the whole of London's press.

Now, Basil was not an experienced lawyer. In fact, his manner was downright irritating. He babbled sentimentally about nature's four-footed friends and the cruelty of stuffing birds and wearing them as ornaments, failing to notice that at least four ladies in the court were adorned with dead birds.

Mr. Williams, the prosecutor, on the other hand, described the case very simply. A horse belonging to and ridden by the Countess of Blackhall had assaulted Lady Jessica. If he had left matters there, Susie would have been found guilty.

But he went on to say that, in his noble client's opinion, the incident had arisen because of the Countess of Blackhall's lower-class background. "Persons from Camberwell," hinted the prosecutor with a sneer, "cannot expect to be versed in the ways of the beau monde."

The magistrate, Sir John Smith, put up his hand to his thin mouth to hide a nasty little smile. For Sir John not only hailed from the middle class, but from Camberwell as well.

He cast a cold eye at the press benches to make sure every one of the ink-stained wretches was listening, and cleared his throat.

"The courts of London," he began in his dry, precise voice, "have more to do with their time than to waste public money settling the squabbles of certain society ladies. I myself have long deplored the use of dead birds as hat ornaments and consider that the horse . . . heh, heh, heh . . . showed remarkable taste. (Laughter in court and frantic and delighted scribbling from the press bench.) 'Persons from Camberwell,' I think you said, Mr. Williams? Dear me, Mr. Williams. The day when I uphold sneers against the middle classes, the backbone of English society, will be a sorry day for British justice.

"Pray, what has Mr. Williams got against Camberwell, that noble borough, that he

178

should state that its people do not know the ways of the beau monde? *The ladies and gentlemen* of Camberwell, like the ladies and gentlemen of any other borough from Hampstead to Kentish Town, are more concerned these days with the state of the nation and the Empire than with the trivial squabbles of a certain section of society who should know better what to do with their position and wealth than to take up the time of this court over such a matter.

"Case dismissed!"

Lady Jessica squawked with rage. Susie looked dizzily around. She had not been asked to say anything. The next case was already being called.

"Don't let the bleeders get yer down," advised a plump and dirty prostitute, giving Susie's arm a squeeze as Susie was led from the court by a triumphant Basil Bryant. "They ain't worth getting your knickers in a knot over."

"Very true," murmured Susie, ever polite.

Susie would very much have liked to leave Basil and go home alone, but Basil jumped into her carriage after her.

"By Jove, Susie!" he cried, patting her knee in a familiar way. "Wasn't I marvelous?"

"Yes," said Susie gratefully, because she

really believed it was thanks to Basil's legal talents that she was a free woman. "Thank you very much. How can I ever repay you?"

"Wait till you get my bill," said Basil with a jolly laugh. Then he leaned forward, gazed intently into Susie's eyes, and said thickly, "Not that I mean to charge *you* anything. 'Pon my soul, no, not a penny!"

"Really, Basil," protested Susie, feeling decidedly uncomfortable under the gaze of his protruding eyes, "you must send me your bill."

Basil tipped his silk hat to one side in what he hoped was a rakish manner and hitched his thumbs into his waistcoat. "We can talk about it later. We're going to be seeing a lot of each other."

"We are?" queried Susie faintly, but Basil was already dreaming of the next day's headlines and then of those future headlines, which would announce, BRILLIANT LAWYER MARRIES LOVELY COUNTESS.

"Oh, dear," said Susie in a whisper.

Giles had arrived too late for the court proceedings. He told himself he was glad. He told himself he didn't really want to see Susie again and turned in the direction of his club. He was walking along Bond

Street when the glitter of a brooch in a jeweler's window caught his eye. He stopped and bent down to look. The brooch was in the shape of a small ptarmigan, an exquisite little thing in gold and rubies. He decided on impulse to send it to Susie as a present.

When he had bought the brooch and given Susie's address for delivery, he began to feel strangely comfortable. It was a very expensive brooch, but he felt obscurely that the price went a little on the way to making amends to the girl.

A red sun was burning down behind the houses into a bank of fog. The lamplighters were already out with their long brass poles to turn the lights of London on.

Smells of food, smells of wine, smells of spices, rose into the smoky air, which already held the exhilarating bite of winter. Carriage lamps bobbed and swayed along the streets. People hurried home from work, packing onto buses, plunging down below to the underground trains, or simply walking, their heels beating out an overture to the London evening.

What a splendid evening to go to the theater, thought Giles. Nothing too clever and nothing too silly. He had it! He would go and see Gilbert and Sullivan's *The Pirates of Penzance* and have dinner at the Troc afterward. He thought perhaps he might call on Susie first — but she might not yet have received the brooch. She might look at him with those large hurt eyes and make him feel like a cad. But he could not help wondering what she was doing.

Susie was trying to cope with Basil Bryant and failing miserably. Lady Matilda had chosen that day of all days to visit an old school friend in Hertfordshire and had said she might stay overnight. Basil was going over and over his success while his eyes roamed a little too freely over Susie's slender body.

They should celebrate, he said. He had it! He would take Susie to see *The Pirates of Penzance*.

Susie had never been to a theater before. She realized that if she said yes, she could take quite a bit of time changing, and that would get her away from Basil, and then after the theater she would firmly shake his hand on the doorstep and send him home. Accordingly she told him she would be delighted.

When she had left the room, Basil put

his thumbs in his waistcoat and gazed around him with smug pleasure. It was a pretty room with its white furniture, long mirrors, and pale-green walls. He liked something a bit more robust himself. He unhitched a thumb and rang the bell.

"Hey, fellow," he said to the liveried footman. "Nip out and buy two tickets for *The Pirates of Penzance*. Money's no object.

"And jump to it!" Basil called gleefully after him, feeling a heady sense of power. It was only a matter of time before he would be master here.

He poured himself a glass of 1830 brandy with a liberal hand and settled back to wait. He suddenly realized that he was not wearing evening dress. He did not want to go all the way to Camberwell. Ah, that magic bell! Another footman appeared, and Basil stared at him with all the amazed pleasure of Aladdin finding out that the lamp really worked.

He pulled out his wallet. "Here, nip round to Henry Brothers in Covent Garden and hire me an evening suit and a set of studs. I'll scribble down my measurements. Hurry back, fellow."

Meanwhile Susie had received the brooch from Giles. She was wearing a severe black opera gown with a high neck and long tight sleeves, a relic of her mourning wardrobe. She hoped it would calm Basil down. She picked up the card and read it again. It simply said, "Best regards, Giles."

She sighed a little. Better not to think of Giles. All he ever did was kiss her and then shout at her and think horrible things about her. Nonetheless she pinned the brooch at the neck of her dress and went slowly and reluctantly downstairs.

Susie did not see Giles at the theater, although he was in an adjoining box. She had eyes only for the stage. She had never enjoyed anything so much in all her life. The colors, the music, the dresses, the sheer delightful nonsense of it all, held her spellbound, while Basil tried to get her attention. And from the shadows of the adjoining box, Giles watched Susie's face instead of the stage.

Giles suddenly felt savagely that *he* should have been the one to give Susie such a treat, not that masher fellow, wherever the hell she had dug *him* up from! He had forgotten, until he saw her again, the stunning allure of her half-childish beauty, her vulnerable femininity, which made her attract him in a way no other woman had ever been able to come near.

There were many women in the theater that night who were much more beautiful, more striking than Susie, but none with that delicate, dreamy charm. He wondered if Helen of Troy had in fact been a quiet, dreamy sort of girl that every man wanted to awaken.

He walked up and down outside his box at the interval, waiting for the couple to come out. He did not want to visit Susie in her box and maybe find out that she was *engaged* to that horrible fellow. He had hoped for a casual encounter.

But Susie, with glimmerings of social awareness, did not want to be seen in company with Basil in the foyer. She was uncomfortably ashamed of his leers and loud voice and perpetually stabbing finger. She did not know what was up with his suit, but his shirt-front snapped and popped every time he leaned forward, and his shoulders seemed to reach down to his elbows.

Giles, patiently waiting for them downstairs after the show, was foiled by a group of giggling debutantes and their predatory parents. By the time he had extricated himself, Susie was gone.

A thickening fog hung over the streets of London as Susie arrived on her doorstep.

She firmly shook hands with Basil, thanked him for the evening, and wished him good night, walking past her butler into the drawing room with a sigh of relief.

She then turned around and found that Basil had trotted in after her.

Susie plucked up her courage. "I must ask you to leave, Basil," she said firmly. "Lady Matilda is not yet back from the country, and I have no chaperon."

"Oh, I'll just stay for a minute," said Basil breezily. "I say, you don't happen to have any more of that brandy?"

Susie rang the bell and ordered the brandy. She decided to have a large one herself, not knowing that the sight of the large measure in her glass sent Basil's evil thoughts soaring. He fortified himself with several large ones and then moved over onto the sofa next to Susie.

"You know, Susie," he said, beginning to breathe heavily, "I'd never have guessed you'd turn into such a seductive woman."

Susie stared down at her glass and said nothing.

Basil edged closer until his thigh was pressed against hers.

"What are you thinking . . . darling?" he breathed.

"I am thinking that I would like to go to

bed," said Susie in a small, chilly voice.

"So would I!" leered Basil. He put down his glass and took hers from her and placed it on the low table in front of them.

"Susie!" he cried, and lunged.

Now, Basil was a virgin, and there is nothing more octopuslike than the mad graspings of the virginal man in a state of high passion. No sooner did Susie manage to claw his hands off one part of her anatomy, when they emerged somewhere else to prod and cling. His mouth was wetly clamped over her own with such vigor that he had managed to cover most of her chin as well. His breath smelled of onions, brandy, and bacon grease from his morning's breakfast, since the cavities of his teeth had retained all the fodder of the day in different stages of decomposition.

Susie finally managed to get in one frantic push. She darted over to the bell and rang it and rang it with such force that the butler and two footmen nearly got jammed in the doorway in their concerted rush.

"Mr. Bryant is just leaving," said Susie.

"Can't blame you," said Basil, winking, his vanity supremely intact. "Phew! Hot stuff, eh? Got a bit carried away myself."

"Please go," said Susie, trying to mask

her feelings of disgust.

"Right-ho!" said Basil cockily. "But I'll be seeing you tomorrow, little girl. It's been a marvelous day. Super evening. Give me something to remember you by, Susie. I know, that brooch."

Susie raised a protective hand to the little brooch and then, with a resigned sigh, unpinned it. She would have given Basil the whole of the crown jewels to take himself off.

Basil cheekily pinned the brooch on the hard front of his rented evening shirt and went off whistling.

Outside, Giles watched him go. Despite the fog, the streetlamp flickered on the brooch on Basil's shirtfront, and Giles felt himself beginning to shake with rage. He had hung around outside for a few minutes before Basil's departure, plucking up his courage to call.

Now he was determined to call.

The butler, knowing his mistress was crying her eyes out in the drawing room, tried to bar his way, but Giles simply pushed him aside.

He hurtled into the drawing room, and Susie raised a pair of tear-drenched eyes to his.

"Oh, Giles!" she sobbed. "Your lovely

brooch. He asked for it, and I was so sick and tired of him that I simply gave it to him to get rid of him." She began to cry again, and Giles sat down beside her and took her hands in his.

His anger had evaporated. She was sick of that fellow, had wanted to be rid of him. That was all that mattered.

"Who on earth was that masher?" he asked.

Susie told him between sobs of Basil and the court case and Basil's grasping, wet lovemaking. "It's always like that," she wailed.

"No, it isn't," said Giles crossly. "I never slobbered over you. Look here, my girl. You'd better marry me."

"Marry *you?*"

"Yes, why not? You're only going to get yourself into trouble. Marry me and come back to the castle."

"I don't know," said Susie wretchedly. "I just want to be left alone."

"That's a fine way to receive a proposal," said Giles huffily. "I don't know if I really want to marry you. I was only thinking of a way to keep you out of mischief."

"Oh!" said Susie in a small voice.

"Mind you," continued Giles, who was in fact beginning to wonder why he had

189

proposed to Susie, "if you prefer to let yourself be mauled about by chappies like Basil Bryant . . ."

"No! I couldn't stand another!" wailed Susie. "I hate Basil. I wish he were dead!"

"I say, steady on," said Giles. "I feel a bit cold when you say that. Here, let me have some of that brandy, and I'll call on you tomorrow, and you can give me your decision."

Basil Bryant walked gaily along the foggy reaches of the Vauxhall Bridge Road. It was the happiest night of his life.

It was also his last.

He had been too exhilarated to climb into a stuffy cab and had decided to walk all the way home to Camberwell. It was in the bag, he decided — fame, fortune, happiness.

He would marry Susie and live happily ever after. What Susie did ever after did not concern him in the least. The fog thinned slightly, and above him a gas lamp sputtered and flared. He stopped to light a cigar, the tiny flame of the match sparking prisms of light from the brooch on his shirtfront.

He tucked his cane under his arm and strolled toward Vauxhall Bridge.

He never knew what hit him. He never felt the grimy fingers tearing at the brooch at his throat, or the harsh breathing of his assailant on his white upturned face.

The shabby villain who had stunned Basil with a convenient beer bottle took the brooch, Basil's wallet, and his watch and chain. Then he felt inside Basil's waistcoat for his heart.

Basil's vanity was indeed the death of him. He had donned a corset for his famous appearance in court. The villain was not used to his young gentlemen victims wearing corsets and therefore could not feel any heartbeat and assumed Basil was dead.

He hitched Basil over his shoulders in a fireman's lift and carried him to the edge of the bridge. Basil slightly regained consciousness in this strange embrace and whispered, "Susie."

It was the last thing he ever said. The next minute, his body hit the cold, filthy waters of the Thames with an almighty splash, and he sank like a stone.

# Chapter Nine

Susie woke up the next morning to find herself a celebrity. Pictures of her covered the front page of every newspaper. She was "The Beautiful Countess." It was just like her dreams, except for one little item in the later editions. The body of Basil Bryant had been dragged from the Thames.

It was as well Basil hadn't lived to read the newspapers. The press called his defense "gauche and amateur." All the photographs were of Susie leaving the court, and Basil was only a shadow in the background. One paper had gone so far as to paint him out.

Lady Jessica was not popular. Society roared with laughter over the exploits of Dobbin and sent cards and invitations to Susie's home. Hostesses vied with each other to see who would be the first to have the mysterious countess as a guest. Gloomily Susie ordered a wreath to be sent to Basil's parents and waited for Giles to call.

But Giles was suffering from a fit of

nerves. When Susie was not actually present, a little of her attraction vanished for him. Then he read of Basil's death in the late editions and felt an almost superstitious qualm.

No sooner did that girl wish someone dead than — bingo! off they up and died.

He decided to remove himself to the country. Having avoided a second marriage for so long, it would be silly to plunge into one now. And just think of her parents! Ten minutes in their company was enough to drive him to a frenzy of boredom.

Susie resolutely refused all invitations and went to Basil's funeral, heavily veiled. Her mother was inclined to be tearful and to promote the late Basil to the right hand of God, until Susie confided to her mama of Basil's amorous assault, at which point Basil fell like Lucifer, cast down into the darkest reaches of the worst hell that Mrs. Burke's fertile mind could devise for him.

The days passed and still Giles did not call. *He probably thinks I murdered Basil,* thought Susie bitterly. *He didn't say he loved me, anyway. He said he wanted to marry me to keep me out of mischief.*

It was not for nothing that Susie was Mrs. Burke's daughter. She banished Giles from her mind as effectively as Mrs. Burke had banished Basil to hell. Then she began to accept some of the invitations.

She was pleasurably surprised. Society was pleasantly surprised with Susie as well. The women found her reassuringly quiet and unassuming, and the men were at first inclined to ignore the shy countess.

But before any of the gentlemen could wake up to Susie's compelling charm, Susie was head over heels in love and engaged to be married.

The lucky man was a widower called Sir Arthur Ireland. Sir Arthur was a tall, thin, ascetic man in his late thirties of a somewhat monkish appearance. He had pale-blue eyes, pale cold hands, and a very thin mouth. His clothes were elegant and his manners perfect. On the day he proposed to her, he kissed her on the cheek with cold, dry lips, and Susie was enchanted with him.

His restraint charmed her. She was delighted with his cold appearance and built all sorts of fantasies around him to explain his reserve. He talked to her at length about politics, old china, food, and furnishings, and Susie drank it all in. When she tried to talk to him, he would wave her to silence. "My dear, when your mind is mature enough to have something to say, then I will listen." And Susie gazed at him humbly and adoringly.

Giles read of her engagement and began to pack his bags. He could not remember being so angry in his life. He did not know whether he was angry with Susie or with himself. Susie had been supposed to wait in London until he, Giles, had made up his mind about her. She was certainly not supposed to go getting herself engaged the minute his back was turned.

He arrived on the day of Susie's engagement party. He had not been invited, but that did not stop him from attending. The public rooms of Susie's mansion were full of guests. The wines and food were of the best. For all her faults, Lady Felicity had trained Susie well. Her household was one of the best run in London.

Giles found Susie and her fiancé in the drawing room, accepting the congratulations of the guests. Giles stood for a moment, surveying Sir Arthur Ireland. He noticed the pale wide eyes and thin mouth. He heard Sir Arthur's dry, condescending laugh and noticed the way he refused to let Susie speak. He was about to walk forward when he was hailed by an old school friend, Harold Blenkinsop. "Hallo, hallo, hallo," said Harold breezily. "Didn't think you'd let that little heiress escape from under your nose."

"Perhaps Sir Arthur has charms that I can't see at this moment," commented Giles dryly.

"Ain't got any as far as I can see," said Harold. "We're all mystified. Y'know, rumor went around when he was married to Margery Mannering that he never laid a finger on her. Fact! I mean, no hanky-panky. Say Margery went to her grave a virgin."

"Must be twaddle," said Giles, but his heart had begun to beat hopefully. He suddenly felt an imperative tug at his sleeve.

"Giles!" hissed Lady Matilda. "You must come through to the conservatory with me. I've got to talk to you."

Giles meekly followed her through to that room, which was at the back of the house. "Now," he said, shutting the glass door behind Lady Matilda and breathing in the hot, damp air, "what's all this about?"

"I never thought she would marry him in a hundred years," wailed Lady Matilda. "I was taken up with a cunning bit of tapestry, and I kept thinking to myself, 'I'll just finish embroidering this bush and then I'll see what Susie's up to,' but, oh dear, one bush led to another bush and then to some tricky roses, and when I finally looked up, there they both were, asking for my blessing.

"But that's not the worst of it. Sir Arthur is said to be desperately in need of money. He only wants her fortune, and she, she's in love with him."

Giles felt a hammer blow over his heart.

"You must elope with Susie this minute," urged Lady Matilda.

"I can't," said Giles crossly. "You say she's in love with this bounder."

"And she's in for a bad shock," said Lady Matilda, dropping her voice to a whisper. "I remember his late wife, Margery, you see. She got a bit tiddly at some house party I was at, and she staggered up to her husband, Arthur, you know, and kissed him full on the mouth.

"Well, he just *looked* at her so, and then he took out his handkerchief and wiped his mouth and threw the handkerchief away, right in front of everyone, and Margery burst into tears and cried, 'You never want to touch me. You never have.' "

"If Susie has a hard time of it, it'll serve her right," said Giles nastily. He could hardly believe that with the glorious Giles around, Susie could actually fall for another man.

"Oh, don't be so pompous," snapped Lady Matilda. "I'm fond of Susie. Go and put a spoke in that bounder's wheel."

"All right," sighed Giles. "I'll try. But Susie is not the easiest of people to talk to. Her mind's always somewhere else."

His heart sank when he saw Susie. She looked absolutely radiant. The Sleeping Princess was in love but had not yet come to life, he thought as he noticed the still-dreamy look in her eyes.

He shook hands with Sir Arthur and managed to edge Susie away into a corner.

"Aren't you happy for me, Giles?" said Susie, laughing. "Oh, I know you said all that rubbish about marrying me, but you only wanted to keep me out of mischief. Arthur will take care of me."

Giles took a deep breath and sent a prayer up to the gods to forgive him for what he was about to do.

"You know, Susie," he said in an urgent whisper, "since your mother's not going to tell you, I had better give you some advice."

"Tell me what?" Susie glanced to where her mother and father were boring a bishop.

"Sir Arthur is a very experienced man, and experienced men don't like cold virgins on their wedding night."

Susie blushed. "I shall not be cold," she said angrily.

"But have you ever really kissed him?" whispered Giles. "A man like that could get very, very tired of just holding hands. Look at him now!"

Sir Arthur had been talking to the notoriously dashing Mrs. Hunter, a redhead of impeccable lineage and doubtful morals. As Susie watched, Mrs. Hunter moved close to Sir Arthur and pressed her left bosom against his austere arm. Susie began to burn with jealousy. Also, Giles's nearness was upsetting her in a way she did not like.

She turned and walked away from Giles to put a possessive little hand on her fiancé's arm. But for once she did not hang on his every word. She was too busy turning various anguished thoughts this way and that. Arthur had never shown the slightest sign of passion. She had been grateful, extremely grateful, for the lack of fumbling and grabbing. She loved when he took her hand in his cold, dry one. Susie felt that there was something almost holy in her love for Arthur, and in that she was almost right.

She abased herself before him, she worshiped his monkish appearance, and hung on his every word.

The more she thought about the idea of exciting Sir Arthur to some display of passion, the more attractive the idea seemed. Arthur was so beautifully remote, so chaste, so withdrawn. Susie was experiencing all the thrills of the hunter, and Sir Arthur, pompously unaware of the Diana that was about to stalk his baser feelings, held forth on the disgraceful state of the British Parliament, implying with every word how much better things would be run if he were in charge.

Susie was so wrapped up in dreams of her campaign, that she had almost forgotten Giles's very existence. Almost, but not quite.

She glanced briefly across the room in his direction and noticed again, in a detached kind of way, that he was extremely handsome. Those tilted eyes of his were glinting down into the eyes of a very pretty girl. Susie felt suddenly sad and cross and wished Giles would go away.

Finally all the guests had gone and Sir Arthur, who was Susie's house guest, was left alone with his fiancée and Lady Matilda. Susie wished Matilda would take her threads and needles and bobbins and stitches and go away and leave them alone. But although she yawned and yawned over her stitchery, Lady Matilda stood her ground.

At last Sir Arthur said good night after placing a chilly kiss on his beloved's brow.

Susie went to her own bedroom, her heart beating hard. Her body ached for Sir Arthur in a pleasurably exciting and quite novel way. She could imagine the feel of his dry fingers against her neck, caressing and stroking.

But Giles's face had an irritating habit of imposing itself on the top of Sir Arthur's body. Damn Giles! She would show him that virgins could be as alluring as experienced women.

Susie, who did not yet know what exactly her virginity was or how it was to be lost, prepared for battle. She mendaciously told Carter she was going straight to bed and, after the door had closed behind the lady's maid, she began to amass her weapons.

She unbraided her hair, which had been pleated by Carter for the night, and brushed it down about her shoulders. She sprayed perfume all over herself and wondered whether to remove her nightgown and look at her naked body in the mirror, but that seemed an incredibly immodest act. The nightgown was of white satin. Susie wished it were black or some daring sort of color. But virginal white it was, and it would have to do.

She picked up a book and sat down to wait until the servants were all asleep. Once or twice her courage nearly failed her. But the memory of Giles's mocking eyes spurred her on.

She began to daydream, and as she built up the dream in her mind, she began to feel more courageous, more fascinating.

She would go to Sir Arthur's bed-chamber and awaken him with a light kiss. His pale eyes would flash fire, and he would gather her in his arms and kiss her tenderly. Susie suddenly remembered the passion she had experienced when Giles had kissed her all that long time ago after the earl had died. Would she feel like that again? If anyone could make her feel that way, it would surely be Sir Arthur.

At last the heavy marble clock on the mantelpiece chimed two. It was now or never.

She put down her book, wrapped her dream more tightly around her, and crept gently along the corridor. With a fast-beating heart, she pushed open the door of Sir Arthur's room.

He was lying on a cane-backed bed with the covers thrown back. The moonlight was streaming in through the open window.

Susie experienced her first qualm of doubt. He was sleeping with his mouth open, and he was wearing a long flannel nightshirt. He had smooth, hairless legs and very large feet.

She lit the gas, which went on with a loud pop, making her jump. She gave a final pat to her hair and approached the bed.

It is very hard to kiss someone who has his mouth wide open, so Susie leaned forward and kissed the tip of his nose.

He made a grumbling noise in his sleep and turned on his side.

Susie looked down at him helplessly. Then she shook his shoulder. He turned around slowly, opened his eyes, and stared at her. Susie stared tremulously back.

He sat bolt upright.

"Ot a oo ooing eah?" said Sir Arthur wrathfully.

Susie thought his face looked funny and odd, but she did not hesitate.

"I am yours, Arthur!" she cried, throwing herself into his arms.

"Et offame!" screeched Sir Arthur, unwinding her arms from around his neck.

He pushed past her, climbed out of the bed, walked over to the marble washstand, and, fishing his teeth out of a glass, popped them into his mouth.

"Now, young lady," he said, clearly and distinctly, "what is the meaning of this?"

Susie was slightly cooled by the fact that her beloved had false teeth. But who was she to demand perfection? She rushed forward again and clutched his thin body to her own vibrant one.

He was cold and rigid; body, arms, face. She rained kisses on his masklike face; she told him she loved him and wanted him.

"Oh, for heaven's sake," said Sir Arthur. "Leave me alone. All this is mawkish and disgusting." He was trembling with distaste and anger. "I thought you were a pure girl."

"But we are to be married!" cried Susie. "We will sleep together." In Susie's innocent mind, sleeping together meant just that.

"Disgraceful! Sickening!" he spluttered. "Let me tell you now, young lady. We shall have separate rooms when we are married. I do not want to be subjected to this animal behavior again."

Lady Matilda removed her ear from the door panel and went to telephone Giles.

"Go to your room this instant!" roared Sir Arthur. "I shall speak to you in the morning."

Susie began to experience some of the fury that hell hath nothing like.

"You're nothing but a dried-up old stick, a mummy," she raged. "What is up with me?"

"You nauseate me," said Sir Arthur cruelly, and then, too late, remembered the Blackhall fortune.

"Oh, my dear," he said, obviously making a tremendous effort, "come to me. You must not take me so seriously."

But now it was Susie who was shuddering with horror and distaste.

"I don't ever want to see you again," she sobbed. "Our engagement is off. I never want to set eyes on you. And take your bloody teeth with you when you go!"

She went out and slammed the door behind her.

Sir Arthur wondered gloomily whether to sue her for breach of promise.

Susie walked along the corridor with shaking legs and down the elegant curved staircase to the ground floor. She had but one thought left in mind — to get as drunk as she possibly could.

With a rare lack of consideration for her

servants, she rang the bell and kept on ringing it, until a disheveled footman appeared and stared in amazement at the sight of his mistress dressed in her nightgown and with her hair down.

"Champagne," said Susie curtly. "Iced. And lots of it."

"Very good, my lady," said the footman gloomily. Just wait till he told the others tomorrow! My lady was turning out to be just as much of a slave driver as the worst of that lot.

After five minutes Susie applied herself to the bell again.

"My lady?" demanded the same footman plaintively.

"The champagne," said Susie feverishly. "Where is it?"

"I'm still chilling it, my lady."

"Bring it up in an ice bucket. *Now!*"

The footman shook his head. As he crossed the hall to the green baize door that led down to the kitchen, he heard someone thumping and pounding on the front door.

"Who is it?" he called through the door.

"The Earl of Blackhall," said Giles, giving the servant the full benefit of his title.

The footman had not been very long in service. Also, he was sleepy and flustered.

He opened the door, and Giles strolled in. "Tell my lady I wish to see her."

"My lady's in the drawing room, but —"

Giles had already opened the door of the drawing room. He stared in amazement at the sight presented by Susie, clad only in a white satin nightgown, with her hair streaming about her shoulders.

"You should not be dressed like that in front of the servants," he said stuffily.

Susie looked quickly up. "Oh, G-Giles," she said with a catch in her voice. "H-he can't *stand* me. And h-he's got false *teeth!*"

"He would," said Giles gleefully. "But what are you doing down here at this time of night?"

"What are *you* doing here at this time of night?" countered Susie suspiciously.

"I was on my way home from a party," lied Giles, "and I saw your drawing room lights on. Anyway, I gather the engagement is off."

"Yes," gulped Susie. "Oh, here's the champagne. I want to get drunk."

"Before you do that," said Giles, waving away the interested footman, "I want to tell you what I'm going to do with you. Now, you have made a sad mess of things up to date, haven't you?"

"Yes, Giles," said Susie, drinking a glass

of champagne quickly and pouring herself another.

"So I suggest I should look after you."

"Why?"

"Why? Because — hey, wait a minute. Leave some of that champagne for me. Three bottles, by George. Did he expect you to drink them all yourself? Because I'm the only person who knows how to look after you, that's why. If you don't marry me, just think what's going to happen to you. Either you're going to have men pawing all over you, or you'll be throwing yourself at them.

"I'll take you off, tonight, to a sort of hunting box thing I've got in Sussex. I'll get a special license and marry you as soon as possible, and after you've been in my arms a few nights, Susie, it should cure you of running after fusty curmudgeons with false teeth."

"Do you love me?"

Giles looked at Susie with some exasperation. He did not want to answer that question yet, even to himself. Lady Matilda had gleefully relayed over the telephone the details of Susie's attempted seduction of Sir Arthur. He had called around immediately. He had discovered that he, Giles, most certainly didn't want any other man to have Susie. He wanted to be the one to introduce her to the delights of love. But whether he loved her or not, he wasn't at all sure.

"I don't know," he said at last. "But I'm prepared to take care of you."

Susie looked at him sadly and a little drunkenly. She suddenly did not want to be left alone anymore.

It would be marvelous to be back at the castle and see Thomson and Mrs. Wight. She could ride Dobbin as much as she wanted, without the half of London staring at her and photographing her. And it had been pleasant to be kissed by Giles. He would not grab or maul.

"I'll let you know in the morning," she said at last, reaching for a fresh bottle of champagne.

"No, now!"

"I'll get Lady Matilda."

"No. You're coming with me — alone."

"Not even Carter?" said Susie in a slightly slurred voice.

"No!"

"Dobbin, then?"

"Your affection for that animal is ridiculous. But, yes, he can travel behind the carriage, and we'll put him on the train."

"I don't think I want to go," said Susie at

last. "I've decided I want to go to sleep more than anything in the whole wide world."

"Look!" said Giles grimly, "Sir Arthur is still on the premises. Do you want to wake up in the morning and find him? Do you think he'll let the Blackhall fortune slip out of his grasp so easily? He'll probably call at *your* bedroom."

Slightly sobered, Susie gave a squeak of alarm.

"Where is this hunting box?" asked Susie.

"It's a quiet little place down in Sussex, near Lewes. Mostly farming country. I don't think it's been used for a hunting party for about eighty years. I've only recently had it put in order. I plan to sell it, but we can use it first."

"Is it small?" asked Susie hopefully, dreams of that cottage beginning to run through her mind.

"Oh, very small."

"All right," said Susie, the champagne making up her mind for her. Also, she had had a young lifetime of obeying orders. How much easier it would be to submit to a stronger will than to go on in this muddle.

"Good girl," said Giles. "Now go and

pack . . . unless you want to travel to Sussex in your nightgown!"

The sleepy footman was summoned again and told to fetch a cab to take them to Victoria Station, where they would catch the Brighton train, stopping at Lewes.

To Giles's surprise, Susie was ready in a remarkably short time. Her bags were strapped up behind the carriage. A snorting and sleepy Dobbin was brought around and tethered to the back. The cabbie was told to drive to Giles's lodgings first, so that he could collect a few belongings, and that being achieved, they clattered through the silent streets in the direction of Victoria Station.

Susie had fallen asleep in the carriage and only awakened when they pulled up in the forecourt of the station.

She climbed stiffly down while Giles fetched a porter. She suddenly did not want to go through with it. Giles appeared like a stern and formidable stranger.

The guard had to be heavily bribed in order to allow Dobbin to share the guard's van, and Giles stood fretting and fuming while Susie whispered soft words in the wretched animal's flattened ears, so that Dobbin would allow himself to be led into his strange quarters.

Susie turned a white face to Giles. She was suffering from an incipient hangover, and nothing seemed quite real — the half-deserted station, the staring porters, and Giles, still in evening dress and opera cloak, looking like some handsome Mephistopheles as he stood by the guard's van with the smoke from a nearby engine billowing about him.

Susie did not want to go. But there was Dobbin, already on the train, and if she did not go, who would look after him?

Giles abruptly made up her mind for her by thrusting her rudely into a first-class compartment and slamming the door behind them both.

The guard waved his green flag, and the London to Brighton express gave one loud cough and shunted forward.

As a pale dawn rose over London they rattled out over the houses, and Susie was reminded vividly of her first journey to Blackhall Castle with the earl. She hoped Giles would not kiss her. But that man seemed to be wrapped up in his own thoughts, and after a bare fifteen minutes he fell sound asleep.

She sat bolt upright for many weary miles, wondering if she had gone mad, wondering how Dobbin was faring in the guard's van, until she too fell asleep.

A steady cold drizzle was falling when the train rolled into Lewes station. Giles woke Susie.

She put her hands to her aching head. Her mouth felt dry and hot, and her brains seemed to be stuffed with cotton wool.

But there was Dobbin to see to, Dobbin to be fussed over, and the sweating and terrified guard to be placated. He said that Dobbin had tried to bite him during the whole journey.

Then there was the cabbie at Lewes station to deal with after Dobbin had kicked the back of his carriage and left scores in the paint. Giles wanted the animal left at the station until he could get a horse box sent for him, but Susie's large eyes filled with miserable tears, and he impatiently gave the cabbie enough gold to buy that gratified man a new hansom.

Finally they jolted off under the shadow of the twelfth-century walls of Lewes Castle, past the cattle pens of the market near the station, and soon they were bowling along a narrow road bordered with high hedges on either side.

Susie tried to keep her spirits up with visions of the hunting box. "Box" sounded reassuringly small. Perhaps they would have a cozy, domestic life. She would cook him meals and smile at him as he smoked his pipe beside the fire in the evening. But Giles did not smoke a pipe. She wondered if she could persuade him to buy one.

"I forgot to leave a note for Lady Matilda!" exclaimed Susie, coming out of her dream.

"I did," said Giles curtly. "She'll know where to find you. We're nearly there."

The carriage had been picking its way for some time down a network of small lanes. It suddenly wheeled around in front of a small lodge.

Giles rapped on the roof. "I'll open the gates, cabbie. There's no one at the lodge."

After opening the gates, he climbed back inside.

The carriage rolled up a long graveled drive bordered on either side by a line of stately elms. After half a mile or so, it came to a stop in front of an imposing mansion.

"Is this the *box?*" asked Susie in surprise.

The hunting box was a trim Georgian manor of red brick, two-storied, and ornamented with a pillared entrance.

"Yes, this is the place," said Giles, sounding more cheerful. "There are hardly any servants, but I keep an elderly couple in residence — Mr. and Mrs. Harrison.

Old Harrison acts as butler when I need him, and Mrs. Harrison sees to the cooking."

Susie's dreams of a country cottage fizzled and died.

The elderly Harrisons were delighted to see their master and his "wife."

"Don't tell them we aren't married," Giles had whispered. "The local vicar is an old school friend of mine, and he should be able to tie the knot pretty soon, so it doesn't matter one way or the other."

Susie nodded weakly, feeling too ill to protest. She was led into a comfortable bedroom on the first floor and collapsed gratefully on a large old-fashioned four-poster bed while Mrs. Harrison, a robust lady in her sixties, unpacked her trunks and lit the fire.

She pulled off Susie's boots, bobbed a curtsy, and left.

Susie was just drifting off to sleep when the door opened and Giles strolled in. He threw his cloak on a chair, took off his jacket, undid his collar and tie and threw them carelessly in a corner, kicked off his evening pumps, and collapsed on the bed next to Susie.

"God, I could sleep for a week," he groaned.

"What are you doing in my bedroom?" cried Susie, sitting up and then moaning as her headache returned in full force.

"It's *our* bedroom," said Giles. "Husband and wife, remember? Now go to sleep."

He turned over on his side and closed his eyes. Susie looked at him doubtfully for a few minutes, but her eyes ached and her head hurt, so at last with a resigned little sigh she too went to sleep.

When she awoke some hours later, Giles had gone.

She climbed stiffly down from the high bed and went to look out of the window. Small chilly flakes of snow were beginning to drift across the bleak countryside. There was a stretch of lawn dotted with old trees in front of the house, ending in a thick wood.

A deer stood frozen at the edge of the wood, looking like a child's toy. Then, with one enormous bound, it disappeared.

A faint smell of cooking drifted up from downstairs. Susie realized she was very hungry indeed.

She bathed and changed and made her way down a beautiful staircase to a bright square hall.

Mrs. Harrison appeared with an enormous white starched lace cap on her gray hair in honor of the occasion.

"My lord is just sitting down to an early dinner, my lady," she said. "If you go straight through to the dining room, you'll just be in time to join him."

She held open a door, and Susie walked into a pleasant room that had not changed much since the days of the Regency. There were no carpets on the highly polished floor. An applewood fire crackled at one end, and the room was lit by two branches of candles on the dining room table.

A silver epergne depicting the Battle of Salamanca dominated the center of the table. Susie sat down and peered cautiously around the battle to where her "husband" was sitting at the other end.

He gave her a brief look and then said, "Move your chair round here, Susie. I can talk to you easier."

Susie went around and sat beside him, looking down at her folded hands, while Mrs. Harrison bustled in with the dishes.

Susie was wearing the brown velvet dinner gown with the bands of sable that she had worn for her first dinner at Blackhall Castle. Giles was wearing a black velvet smoking jacket with plaid trousers and an open-necked soft white silk shirt and a paisley cravat with a small ruby stickpin.

Susie thought he looked very handsome but very Bohemian. He should have at least put on a dinner jacket.

Unconventional clothes could be taken off so quickly, she reflected, and then blushed at her unconventional thought.

"I rode over to see the vicar, Charlie Wade," said Giles, shaking out his napkin. "Then I went into Lewes and arranged a special license. Charlie can marry us in a couple of days time. He thinks the whole thing is a great laugh."

"He does?" asked Susie miserably. She had been hoping for a severe cleric who would have pointed out to Giles the error of his ways.

Susie was wishing desperately she had not come.

But she was young and she was hungry, and she attacked her meal with a good appetite, refusing, however, Giles's offer of champagne.

She felt she never wanted to touch the stuff again.

Giles suddenly wondered what to talk about. He had never really *talked* much to Susie that he could remember.

"Dobbin's all right," he said at last. "Ate a good dinner."

"Oh, thank you," said Susie, her beautiful eyes lighting up with real gratitude. "Is his stable warm enough?"

"Yes."

There was another silence.

"It's a very pretty house," ventured Susie at last. "I did not think a hunting box would be so big."

"Well, it has to be," Giles pointed out. "Where else would one put one's guests?"

There was another silence while the wind howled miserably outside and the snow whispered against the windowpanes.

"Port?" asked Giles after the dishes had been cleared and an old fashioned sort of tray on wheels containing port, Madeira, and liqueurs to have with walnuts had been wheeled onto the table.

"No. Yes. I mean, thank you, I would like some," said Susie miserably, her eyes falling before the gleam that was appearing in the blue eyes opposite.

She drank a glass of port very quickly. "What shall we do this evening?" she asked brightly.

"What do you think?" asked Giles with some surprise.

Susie blushed a painful red. "Aren't you going to wait until after the wedding?"

"No."

"Oh."

There was another silence.

Susie drank several glasses of port in quick succession. She hoped to encourage Giles to drink, so that he would fall asleep, but although he was drinking quite steadily, he looked remarkably bright-eyed and sober.

At last he said, "I think we should go to bed now, Susie."

"I'll just finish my —"

"I said *now!*"

"Oh, must we? Oh, dear. Oh, very well," sighed Lady Blackhall.

# Chapter Ten

"What did you say, Giles?"

"Necrophilia."

"What's that?"

"Never mind," sighed Giles. "Go to sleep."

Susie turned over on her side and hunched herself up into a small ball, drawing her legs up against her chest. What had she done wrong? But it had all been so painful and bewildering.

First he had insisted on undressing her, which had taken an agonizingly long and embarrassing time.

He had unfastened the brown velvet dress, then the camisole blouse, then the layers of petticoats tied with tape at the waist. Then he had unbuttoned her long frilly knickers and unclipped her stockings from their garters. Swearing mightily, he had wrestled with the metal busks of her corset until he had got them undone, and then had stared in dismay as she stood revealed in all the glory of her fine wool combination, a one-piece garment that covered her from her bust to her knees.

He had started to laugh, and that had been horrible. "Honestly, Susie darling," he had cried, "how can you females possibly wear so many clothes?"

She had simply stood there, like a statue, staring at him, wide-eyed. He had started to take off his own clothes, and that was when she had found the courage to ask him to blow out the candles, which he had done with an indulgent smile.

As he had carried her to the bed and had started to remove her one last garment, remembering from his long experience that it unfastened by a sort of back panel over the bottom, she had closed her eyes tightly.

He had started to kiss her, and that was all right, warm and comforting. He had kissed her and caressed her for a very long time, and then, all at once, a lot of very painful and embarrassing things had started to happen.

He had not seemed to realize how painful it was and had answered every one of her moans with a moan of passion. Just when she thought she simply could not bear it any longer, he had collapsed on top of her.

She had lain supporting his body for some minutes and then had asked timidly,

"Is it all over?" At which Giles had turned his back on her and had muttered that word that she did not understand.

Giles closed his eyes and willed sleep to come. That "Is it all over?" of hers had been like a jug of cold water. She had endured his embraces, that was all. He had made a simply terrible mistake. But now he would have to marry her.

He tried to remember his first nights with his ex-wife, but found he could not remember much except his surprise that she had seemed so experienced. He began to wonder if he had ever slept with a virgin before and after a lot of long and painful thought, decided he had not.

He felt the beginnings of some pity for Susie and some understanding. But, at that moment anyway, he did not feel he could touch her again.

He tried manfully to woo her on the days and nights before their wedding, but she only submitted reluctantly to his embraces, looking at him with hurt eyes, like a dog who wonders why his master is beating him but is heartbreakingly determined to endure anything in the cause of love and duty.

They were married on a grim, dark day

in a tall, narrow church in the neighboring town of Whiteboys. The weather was so cold and bitter that only a few of the townspeople had turned out to cheer the couple, and the only guests invited were the Harrisons, who had finally been told that the couple had not been married before after all.

The vicar, Charlie Wade, was a muscular, jolly man with a hearty, jovial laugh and a pretty, silly wife, who managed to play the organ and cry copiously at the same time all through the service.

The vicar and his wife were invited to the wedding breakfast and stayed for the whole day, determined to make the most out of this rare social occasion.

At last they left, and Susie, Lady Blackhall for the second time, was left alone with her husband.

"Susie," said Giles gently after the Harrisons had cleared the dishes and retired, "you must be patient. You do not seem to enjoy my lovemaking at the moment, but I feel sure that pleasure will come with time. Do you love me?"

"I don't know," said Susie miserably, tying her napkin into a knot.

Now, this was exactly the answer that Giles had given her, but he felt very angry indeed. She might at least have lied.

He tried to fight it, but his bad temper got the better of him.

"You're not even *trying*," he said severely.

"I *am* trying," said Susie, stung to the quick. "Night after night. It *hurts*, Giles."

"That's because you won't let yourself relax."

"Why is it always my fault?" said Susie, beginning to sob.

"Oh, for God's sake, stop being such a wet blanket. All right. Hear this, my lady. I will not sleep with you again until you go down on your knees and *beg* me."

"Don't be silly," said Susie, feeling a burst of healthy anger. "Beg *you?*"

"Yes, beg me, you frigid little snow maiden. Furthermore, this was supposed to be our honeymoon. But I'm damned if I'm going to stay here, with you mooning around like a bloody martyr. I'm going back to the castle tomorrow. I've got work to do there, which, I may add, is more rewarding than any of the hours I've slaved over your cold body."

"How dare you!" cried Susie, her cheeks flaming. "You are no gentleman, sir!"

"Who ever heard of playing ladies and gentlemen between the sheets?"

"Crude, vulgar, awful —"

"Shut up! I made a mistake, and now I'm stuck with you. For Christ's sake, take your miserable face out of here. You make me sick."

"Not half as sick as you make me," screamed Susie, desperate to hurt him as much as he had hurt her. "You, with your grabbing hands and wet mouth. Men! You're all the same!"

"Only after one thing," he sneered.

"Exactly!"

"At least there are plenty of women to supply that one thing," said Giles. "You supply nothing, d'ye hear? Nothing! Neither conversation, nor company, nor affection, nor love. All you care about is that mangy horse of yours."

"Perhaps because Dobbin loves me," said Susie, suddenly quiet.

"Oh, go away," said Giles wearily. "I'm going to get drunk."

Susie stalked from the room, her head held high, and Giles sat and nursed his port and a guilty conscience. He had not meant to be so cruel, but that untouchable air about her drove him mad.

The unhappy couple settled in for the long winter at Blackhall Castle.

They exchanged chilly presents at

Christmas and a chilly kiss, and apart from that, they did not have much to do with each other.

Their bitter atmosphere affected even the servants, who became quarrelsome and split up into two camps, one led by Mrs. Wight, favoring Giles, and the other led by Thomson, favoring Susie.

As far as Susie was concerned, she had had her taste of reality. Better to retreat to the safe world of her dreams, where that tan and handsome and *kindly* man was always waiting for her.

Giles bitterly noticed her vague and dreaming air of abstraction, and it infuriated him more than her cold snubs had done.

It was when he was glancing through the social columns that he hit upon an idea.

Winter had at last fled, and the days were growing warmer and longer. Thoughts of old romances and old conquests began to burn in his blood. He was determined to show Susie somehow that he was still considered a highly attractive and desirable young man. And Mary Bartlett had returned to London. Mrs. Bartlett, an old amour of Giles's, had long been called The Merry Widow. She was a voluptuous redhead with a large fortune and a roving eye.

He would hold a house party, nothing too elaborate, just a few couples and the intriguing Mrs. Bartlett.

Susie accepted the news of the house party with infuriating calm. She ordered flowers to be arranged, wrote menus for the dining room and cards for the doors of the guest rooms, and dreamed of that handsome, square, solid man who would arrive and rescue her from Giles's icy scorn.

The Earl and the Countess of Blackhall were standing on the castle steps, arm in arm and with fixed social smiles pinned on their faces, to greet the first guests.

Giles searched the arriving carriages and motorcars anxiously for Mrs. Bartlett, and Susie searched for her dream lover.

They both arrived at once.

A smart, brand-new Lanchester painted a dazzling shade of pink rolled up after the other guests had arrived. Clashing magnificently with the paintwork of her automobile was the flaming red hair of Mrs. Bartlett. Only she wasn't Mrs. Bartlett anymore.

"I've just got married, darling," she cried, pressing Giles to her ample bosom. "Isn't he a poppet? I'm Lady Mary Glassop now. This is my husband, Jimmy."

Sir Jimmy Glassop was a wealthy financier, one of the new kind of aristocracy who had turned from their lands to make their fortune in trade. He was tall and handsome with a square, tanned face, and honest brown eyes. He had walked straight out of Susie's dreams, and she could not take her eyes off him.

Giles watched her over Lady Mary's lace shoulder and felt that his superb plan was backfiring.

Lady Mary linked her arm familiarly in Giles's and called over her shoulder to her husband, "See that the servants know where to put my bags, darling." She went into the castle, talking animatedly to Giles. She had not even looked at Susie.

Susie turned to Sir Jimmy and gave him a radiant smile. "If you will come with me," she said, "I will show you to your rooms."

"I say," said Sir Jimmy. "We haven't been introduced."

"I'm Susie, Giles's wife," said Susie, leading the way.

"He's married!" exclaimed Jimmy, lumbering after her. "There was nothing about it in the social columns. Giles married! Well, well, well."

Susie conducted him up to the top of the

keep and into a guest suite of rooms, which was in fact Giles's former quarters. He had moved into the earl's rooms, and Susie had taken up the adjoining suite, which had been redecorated in her honor. Jimmy thanked her heartily and said he would go straight back downstairs again and join his wife, since the trunks had all been safely bestowed.

Susie trotted along happily beside him. When they reached downstairs again, it was to be informed by a disapproving Thomson that my lord and my lady had gone walking down by the lake.

"Do you want to join them?" asked Susie.

"No, my dear," said Jimmy. "I simply want to sit down and stretch my legs and have something to drink."

She led him into the rose chamber and ordered Thomson to supply the necessary refreshment.

"Do you mind if I smoke my pipe?" asked Jimmy, taking a venerable meer-schaum from his pocket.

"Oh, no!" sighed Susie adoringly. "I adore men who smoke pipes."

Jimmy looked at her in surprise. "Giles smoke a pipe?"

"No."

"Oh," said Jimmy, looking startled and then looking closely at Susie for the first time.

She was wearing a white lace tea gown threaded with gold silk ribbons. Her hair was dressed low on her forehead in the latest fashion, and the style accentuated the size of her large eyes. He watched the play of her heavy lashes against her cheek and felt a little quiver of surprise. *By George!* he thought. *I've charmed this little lady.*

"Do you come up to town often?" he asked.

"No," said Susie. "I have a house there, you know, but I haven't visited it since I was married. Giles's Aunt Matilda lives there at the moment."

"Season'll soon be starting," he commented, puffing on his pipe and looking at her admiringly through the clouds of aromatic smoke. "Young thing like you should be going to all the balls and parties."

"I don't really like balls and parties," said Susie. "I like a quiet country life."

"So do I," said Jimmy, "but I can't talk my wife into it. She likes the social round. Before I had any money, I lived in my parents' old home down in the country. It was very small and quiet, but I rather liked it. Good hunting."

"I sometimes think I would like a small house," said Susie, thinking of that thatched cottage. "Do you have a dog?"

"Whole pack," he said amiably.

"I mean a pet dog," urged Susie, thinking of the dog called Rover who would gambol about the garden.

"No," he said. "I like dogs in the kennels, where they belong. Nasty, smelly things to have about the house, you know. Hair all over the cushions and bones under the carpets."

Susie sighed. Nobody was perfect.

She heard a trill of laughter and turned her head. Mary was entering, hanging onto Giles's arm. She was rather on the heavy side, but she had magnificent skin and eyes as blue as Giles's own. She was wearing a silk chiffon dress, which Susie noticed was cut so tightly to her voluptuous figure that it was almost possible to read the name of her corsetiere.

"Giles has been telling me he's *married*. Fancy that. Our gay bachelor tied down at last! Lucky girl," she cooed at Susie and then raised her penciled eyebrows as she intercepted the cold look that passed between Susie and her husband.

In the days that followed, Susie was quite happy, however, to see Giles's attention so much taken up with Lady Mary. It left Jimmy plenty of time to pay attention to her.

The members of the house party — who were a surprisingly middle-aged lot, Giles not wanting any masculine competition — passed the time pleasantly enough, walking and picnicking, gossiping, and playing parlor games and practical jokes. Finally, one by one, they left, but Lady Mary and her husband stayed on.

Susie received an anxious letter from her parents, which had been forwarded from her London address. They had heard rumors that Susie was married again. Surely that could not be the case, since she would have asked her beloved parents to the wedding. Lady Matilda had been quite *furtive* and had said that Susie was traveling *abroad*. Now, didn't Susie ever stop to think of how her parents longed to travel? And so on.

Susie felt a pang of guilt. She did not want her parents to know she was married, for they might then be spared the horror of ever finding out that she had become divorced. For the more Giles flirted with the all-too-willing Lady Mary, the more Susie wound Jimmy into her dreams and thought her life would be perfect if only she could be married to *him*.

Susie and Jimmy went for long companionable walks together, Susie for once in her life doing most of the talking while Jimmy puffed amiably on his pipe and put in an odd word or two.

Giles kept a cynical eye on Susie. He was shrewd enough to know that Jimmy was too much of a gentleman to contemplate even flirting with Susie, but he could not help feeling fiercely jealous. She was his property, after all.

Susie would not even admit to herself that she was bitterly hurt by Giles's light flirtation with the gorgeous Lady Mary. Every time Lady Mary would lay a caressing hand on Giles's arm, Susie would wince and burrow deeper into her dreams, until she saw the outside world through a vague haze.

She desperately wanted security. She wanted a strong man to look after her. As the seductive, warm spring days slipped by, she became more than ever convinced that that man was Jimmy.

The two couples dined and played cards together, Lady Mary and her husband joking and laughing, and Giles and Susie subdued and quiet.

Lady Mary was quick to notice that

Giles only flirted with her when Susie was around, and settled down to enjoy the game. The fact that Susie might be getting hurt by this by-play did not trouble Mary in the least. Although she was not a cruel woman, she was shallow and thrived on the jealousy of other women.

There is nothing like long, drawn-out adolescence for causing mild insanity — the type of insanity where one thinks one is terribly sane.

And so Susie decided that Jimmy loved her. He needed encouragement. He was only waiting for a word from her.

She started to plan to get him to herself for the day.

She knew he was in the habit of riding early and strolling about the garden. She went in search of him one dazzling morning while the dew was still heavy on the grass.

Jimmy was strolling down by the lake. He paused to admire the heavy purple blossoms on the lilac tree and noticed the stone bench next to it. He sat down and was just beginning to light his pipe when he heard the patter of footsteps on the path and looked up in surprise.

Susie came tripping toward him, looking very much part of the spring morning in a pale-green organza dress, which fluttered around her ankles as she walked.

"Hey, Susie," said Jimmy amiably, getting to his feet. "Early riser, just like me."

"Yes," said Susie. "We have a lot in common."

She peeped up at Jimmy through her lashes to see if the point had struck home, but he was gazing placidly at a family of ducks paddling across the smooth surface of the lake.

He searched in his pocket, took out a tin of tobacco, and rattled it ruefully. "Empty," he said. "Better drive into Barminster and get myself some more."

"I thought of going into town myself," said Susie casually and waited for him to invite her to come along.

"Good," he said, "that'll save me a trip. That is, if you wouldn't mind picking up a quarter pound of Embassy for me. It costs two shillings, and you should be able to get it at Hadden's in the High Street."

Susie's face fell, "I thought perhaps you might drive me into town."

"Glad to." He looked at her in some surprise. "Tell you what, you fetch Giles, and I'll get Mary, and we'll make an outing of it. I'll stand you all lunch at the Crown."

Emboldened by her dreams, Susie

plunged in. "Couldn't we just go together?" she asked. "I think Giles is still asleep, and Mary doesn't ever get up before noon, as you know."

"All right," said Jimmy equably. "We'll take the motor, and that way we'll be back before they even wake up."

Susie turned her head to hide a frown. Once Jimmy found out she loved him, then he would surely be in no mood to hurry back.

They pottered amicably enough down the High Street under the flapping blinds of the little shops. Susie was thinking of some way she could get Jimmy to herself and away from the crowds for a little bit. She wished she knew something about motor engines, so that she could sabotage the motor, but even if she could, Jimmy would probably go in search of a mechanic.

Jimmy bought his tobacco, and Susie bought ribbons and laces and a length of material she did not really want.

While the shopkeeper was wrapping up her purchases, Susie sat on a hard wooden chair beside the counter and racked her brains for somewhere quiet to take Jimmy.

"There you are, my lady," said the shopkeeper breezily. "Gorgeous day. I'll be taking the missus out in the carriage for a bit of air like this evening, if the weather stays fine. There's a lovely little spot down by the River Bar near an old ruined folly. Used to be part of Lord Humfry's estate, but now it belongs to Farmer Briggs, and he don't mind people strolling around. Really lovely it is this time of year, my lady."

"I would like to see it," said Susie with such urgency that the shopkeeper stared at her in surprise. "We have a motor. Which route do we take?"

"Well, my lady, you go to the end of the High Street and turn along Minster Road till you gets to Hackett's Crossing. Take Parson's Lane about a mile or so and you'll come to a big pair of stone gateposts with sort of eagles on top. There's a track through there, broad enough for a motor, which'll take you down to the river."

"What do you say?" asked Susie, looking up at Jimmy with shining eyes.

"I suppose it wouldn't take too long. Perhaps I'd better telephone Mary and —"

"Oh, no, that won't be necessary," said Susie hurriedly. "We'll just take a quick look."

"Righty-ho," replied Jimmy with his usual amiability.

Outside, Susie sat back in the shocking pink car while Jimmy took the wheel and steeled herself for the scene to come. Of course, at first he would probably feel he had to say he was fond of Mary, but after that — well, love would conquer all. Then all they had to do was escape to that cottage where the birds always sang in the thatch and the dog, Rover, was waiting at the gate.

They found the road to the River Bar easily enough, turning in through the stone gateposts and bumping along a rutted track to the folly by the river. Jimmy switched off the engine.

It was indeed a beautiful spot.

A moss-covered ruin of a folly stood on a little knoll above the river, which foamed and sparkled over its bed of silver pebbles. The sun slanted in great shafts through the translucent spring leaves of the trees, and the warm air was heavy with the smells of flowers and grass.

Susie was content to sit drinking in the silence and the nearness of Jimmy, warm, friendly, and reassuring from the homely smell of his tobacco to the rough hair of his tweeds.

"There's your river," said Jimmy cheerfully. "Now you've seen it, and very pretty it looks. Better be getting back."

He made a move as if to start the car, but Susie put her little gloved hand over his.

"Please, Jimmy," she said softly. "Walk with me for a little. There's something I have to tell you."

"Righty-ho," said Jimmy. "But better make it quick."

They climbed down from the car. Susie walked around and linked her arm in Jimmy's, and they strolled down to the edge of the river. She was wearing a dashing white straw bonnet lined with green silk, which she knew became her.

"Now," said Jimmy questioningly, turning to look down at her.

Susie took a deep breath. "Jimmy, I feel that the regard I have for you is deepening into something stronger."

"Oh, I say," bleated Jimmy, but Susie had the bit between her teeth and could not be checked. She went on in a rush, looking up into his bewildered brown eyes and hanging onto his arm.

"We both want to live in the country. We're not socialites like Giles and Mary. We could easily get divorces. People do quite a lot these days. We could buy a cottage like the one I told you about. Oh,

Jimmy darling, I can see it now! You can smoke your pipe in the evenings in the garden, and I will lean on the back of your chair. I saw some lovely chintz for curtains just the other day. And I could have a dog, a dog called Rover. I know you said you didn't like dogs, but I feel you were only chaffing me. We were *made* for each other, Jimmy. Jimmy?"

Jimmy stared down at her with his mouth open. Then he gently disengaged himself from her grasp and, taking out a large handkerchief from his cuff, proceeded to mop his face.

Suddenly a look of comprehension dawned on his pleasant face. "I say, old girl, it's the damned sun plus an open motorcar. Hat's not enough in this weather. Same thing happened to Mary once at Antibes. Got very tetchy, she did, and started babbling the most awful nonsense. Now, not another word until I get you back home."

"But, J-Jimmy —"

"Sun, that's what it is," he said soothingly, leading her firmly back to the Lanchester and all but shoving her into the seat. "Sun's very strong this time of year. Dear me."

He set the motor in motion, and they

lurched off back down the path.

Susie sat as far away from him as she could, hunched up and miserable. He hadn't understood her! He *must.*

The noise of the engine made conversation impossible. Jimmy broke the speed record all the way back to the castle, hurtling round the bends at a dizzying forty miles an hour.

He pulled up at the entrance to the keep and, before Susie could open her mouth, he had sent a footman to fetch Carter, and in the next breath had gone bounding upstairs, calling for his wife.

Susie dismissed Carter as soon as she got to her sitting room and sat down by the window and put her head in her hands.

What had gone wrong?

Suddenly through the open window she could hear the chatter of voices coming from Jimmy's rooms.

Susie was a well-brought-up girl. She knew that to eavesdrop was wrong. But perhaps, just perhaps what she had said to Jimmy had finally struck him and he was, even now, asking his wife for a divorce.

She crept out into the corridor and along toward their rooms, the voices becoming louder as she turned the bend in the stone corridor.

Then she stood stock still. Lady Mary was laughing fit to burst.

"Do stop laughing, Mary, and listen," Jimmy could be heard saying in a pleading voice. "It was the most bloody awful thing to happen. Touched in her head with the heat, she was. Babbling on about how we would live in a country cottage with a dog called *Rover.*"

"Oh, my poor lamb!" gasped Lady Mary. "How on earth am I going to keep my face straight this evening? We'd better leave at once."

"And I thought she was such a nice little thing," grumbled Jimmy.

"Hidden fires, my dear. Hidden fires," said Mary, laughing. "It's that comfortable tweedy look of yours, Jimmy. It gets all the girls."

"Aren't you a bit jealous?" complained Jimmy.

"Of a silly little girl? Nonsense! I'm sorry for Giles all the same. He could do with something with a bit more flesh and blood."

"What are you doing?"

"I'm taking your nasty hot shirt off to soothe the savage breast."

"Oh, darling. No, don't stop. Do that again."

Susie walked along the corridor with her face flaming and her legs shaking. Her dreams lay around her feet in tinsel ruins, and she was left shivering and alone with the horrid reality of the present world.

# Chapter Eleven

Giles walked along beside the lake in a worried frame of mind. Jimmy and Mary had just made a very abrupt and strange departure. Mary had been inclined to giggle a lot and look sly, and Jimmy had looked as embarrassed as a man could be.

Susie was nowhere to be found.

He didn't know what to do about Susie. All his flirting with Mary had left her unmoved, and he hadn't liked the way she had looked at Jimmy. Now, why had Jimmy looked so embarrassed? His heart began to hammer. She wouldn't, she couldn't . . .

Suddenly, to his rage, he saw Dobbin strolling along the path toward him. Susie let that bloody animal roam at will like a pet dog.

Giles glared at Dobbin, and Dobbin flattened his ears and glared back.

"You mangy lump of catsmeat," grated Giles. "Why don't you stay in the stables or run in the pasture or just be somewhere where a horse is supposed to be?"

Dobbin sneered down his long nose,

cropped a lilac blossom, and stood glowering at Giles with the blossom hanging nonchalantly from his mouth. He looked remarkably like a sulky gigolo.

"Well, I am going to find your mistress, and from now on you are to be locked in the stables when you are not being exercised. Look at you! You're the nastiest-looking thing on four legs I've ever seen."

He turned his back on Dobbin and stared across the lake.

Now, Dobbin was a thoroughly spoiled horse. He turned to go, looking back at Giles over his plump, overfed shoulder. Giles's well-tailored back irritated Dobbin's small, mean brain more than Giles's face had done.

He lashed out with his hoof and kicked Giles smartly in the seat of the pants. Giles went sailing off into the lake, and Dobbin cantered off with a whicker that sounded remarkably like a laugh.

Gasping and spluttering, Giles hauled himself to the shore. He looked wildly around, but there was no sign of Dobbin. He returned to the castle and changed his clothes and then, jerking a riding crop out of the stand in the hall, he went in search of Dobbin. The wretched animal was nowhere to be found.

Gradually his temper cooled and he began to worry about Susie. He hadn't seen her all day. And why, why, why had Jimmy looked so embarrassed?

Then Giles remembered the bluebell wood that sloped down to the sea about half a mile from the castle.

He found Susie sitting on the springy grass at the top of the cliff. She was sitting with her feet stretched out in front of her and looking down at her hands.

He went up quietly and sat down beside her.

She turned and looked into his eyes. He stared at the pain and bewilderment there, and then his heart began to quicken. For all her distress, he felt that Susie was really looking at him for the first time.

Giles was about to ask her if he could shoot her horse, and in the same breath he was about to accuse her of having an affair with Jimmy.

But he took a deep breath and put a companionable arm around her shoulders.

"Mary and Jimmy have gone," he said at last.

"You will miss Mary," said Susie in a small voice.

"And you will miss Jimmy," said Giles.

Susie blushed painfully. "I don't know,"

she said. "Perhaps it will be pleasant to have the place to ourselves for a change."

Giles felt instinctively that the time had come to make one last effort.

"I only flirted with Mary to make you jealous, Susie. And I suppose that's why you flirted with Jimmy?"

"Oh, yes," lied Susie thankfully. "Yes, that must have been it."

He pulled her head gently back until it rested on his shoulder and began to stroke her hair. The long bitter winter might never have existed.

Susie was suddenly overwhelmed with gratitude for Giles — for being so gentle, for letting her save face. Giles was so much more worldly and sophisticated than she that surely he must have guessed at her mad fiasco with Jimmy. Susie would have been very surprised indeed had she known that he hadn't the faintest idea of what had actually happened and would have been in quite a vicious rage had he known that she had declared her love for another man.

He bent his fair head and dropped a kiss on her nose, and she stared up into those strangely tilted eyes. Susie all of a sudden wanted to make up to him for all her snubs and days of neglect. She twisted and wound her arms around his neck and kissed him full on the mouth. His lips burned and clung to hers, and he felt the answering passion in her body with a dawning surprise. This time, he was determined not to frighten her, so he contented himself with kissing her passionately on the mouth, over and over again.

Susie's body began to feel hot, and she was aching and trembling with a sort of terrible sweetness, and suddenly kissing was not enough.

She shyly unbuttoned Giles's shirt and kissed his chest, and for Giles, all the world went mad. "Let's move out of sight," he gasped when he could.

It may seem impossible to make love to an elegantly dressed young lady on a sloping cliff in the middle of a lot of bluebells, but Giles managed superbly. For Susie, the lovemaking that had begun as a way of making amends ended in ecstasy as she answered all his passion with new-minted passions of her own, oblivious of sharp pebbles digging into her back and blissfully unaware that all her multiple layers of clothing were now spread far and wide among the bluebells.

The sun had long set over the sea by the time they made their slow and exhausted way back to the castle, dreamily hanging on to one another.

As they approached the castle walls a great, hulking black shape detached itself from the deeper blackness of the walls and loomed over them.

Susie gave a little scream and then laughed. "Oh, it's only poor old Dobbin. Dear, dear precious. I shall find you some sugar as soon as I get home. Did poor Dobbin miss me?"

The silly horse bent his head and nuzzled her hand.

A full moon rose over the castle and shone down on Susie's face as she looked up at Giles.

"Don't you just *adore* Dobbin?" she asked.

Giles looked down at her radiant face and into her eyes, which were alight with love and remembered pleasure.

"Oh, yes," he lied stoutly. "Splendid beast!"

Love is a wonderful thing.

The employees of Thorndike Press hope you have enjoyed this Large Print book. All our Large Print titles are designed for easy reading, and all our books are made to last. Other Thorndike Press Large Print books are available at your library, through selected bookstores, or directly from us.

For information about titles, please call:

(800) 223-1244
(800) 223-6121

To share your comments, please write:

Publisher
Thorndike Press
295 Kennedy Memorial Drive
Waterville, ME   04901